DEAD PLANET

THREE TALES OF INVASION

JOSEPH PESAVENTO

This is a work of fiction. Names, characters,
places, and incidents are either the product of the
author's imagination or are used fictitiously.
Any resemblance to actual persons, living
or dead, events, or locales is entirely coincidental.

Dead Planet Copyright © 2023 Joseph Pesavento

All rights reserved. No part of this book may
be reproduced or used in any manner without
written permission of the copyright owner except
for the use of quotations in a book review.

Cover & Interior Design by Scott Cole
(www.13visions.com)

To Nadia. You ground me even in space.

FROM THE DEPTHS OF SPACE

The void of space was the sole view for the crew aboard the *Sempiternal*. The glow from the controls was barely noticeable anymore. Randall, the ship's pilot, stepped in front of the main window to look down upon Earth.

"Navigator, how much longer until we reach Earth?" Randall asked.

"Seven days, three hours, and eleven minutes until we enter the Earth's atmosphere. Is there anything else I can help you with, Randall?" Navigator asked.

Navigator was the highly intelligent operating system controlling *Sempiternal*. Not only did it provide the obvious coordinates for any destination, but it was the crew's source for transmissions, onboard controls, and an endless music playlist that kept them all sane for the duration of their mission.

"That is all for now. Thank you."

Macy approached Randall, wrapping her arm around his waist. She leaned her head against his shoulder blade.

"Better than any honeymoon we could have chosen, my captain." She gently kissing Randall's arm.

Randall swung his arm behind her, pulling her close to his side.

"Well, in about a week, we can go anywhere down there we want. No need to be on this ship again for a long time."

Carter approached Randall and Macy, scoffing at their intimacy.

"I could use a break from all this PDA." He sat at the table and fiddled with a small piece of machinery.

Macy leaned over the table, shooting Carter a look.

"This ship is small, but you've had your private quarters. Relax." Macy walked back to the main window.

Carter continued with his fiddling. He was easily silenced when he had gear to fix.

Randall stood beside Macy, gazing at Earth as if it were their retirement party calling to them.

The ship rocked back and forth, throwing him off balance. Macy braced herself against the frame of the window, and Carter dropped the machinery he was working on to brace himself at the table.

"This ship can't even stand space anymore," Carter said sarcastically.

"Was that gravitational pull?" Macy asked.

"Most likely not. I think we are still too far out for that," Randall said.

Gunther entered the room from the hallway. He approached Randall as he held on to the walls for support.

"It's as if we're in a gravity pull, but we're too far from any planet or moon for that."

"Hey, guys. Look at this." Macy pointed with a troubled expression on her face.

As the rest of the crew moved toward the main window, a small black hole opened slowly in the distance. A large vessel crept out from the expanding hole, emerging to reveal its size, dwarfing the *Sempiternal*. It was black sections of chrome that reflected the sun. The edges grew visible while it emerged further from another side of space.

"Look at the size of that thing," Macy said.

"Is that showing up on radar?" Randall asked.

Gunther looked at the controls to see the radar blank. Satellites often appeared on the radar, but not the ship that dwarfed the *Sempiternal*.

"Nothing. Makes no sense."

The team gathered around the main window and watched the rest of the ship emerge from the black hole. It hovered above Earth, spanning the entire width of the planet. The black hole closed, almost as if it were shut with a remote, as the ship aligned with Earth.

Carter searched the controls, pressing a series of buttons. He grew frustrated. "Too bad we don't have any guns on this ship."

"Even if we did, we can't scratch that thing," Randall said. "Let's just wait and see what happens."

The colossal vessel remained still and then a light beamed out from the bottom. The crew turned away from the blinding flare, and when they looked back, they saw a tiny figure floating down toward the surface.

"Is that... Is someone coming out of the ship?" Gunther asked.

"It's not a telegram, buddy," Carter scoffed. "Whoever that is, let's just hope they aren't hostile."

"Not who, but what. That thing is glowing," Macy said.

The figure had a faint purple aura. As it closed in on Earth, the aura pulsed with intensity. Thankfully, the figure stopped after several seconds of descension. Then the pulsing became rapid and the purple aura brightened. A flash emitted from the figure.

When Randall looked back to the colossal ship, it was gone, having left the glowing figure behind. A smaller ball appeared below the figure, hovering there and growing nearly twice its size, and glowing just as brightly.

"The ship's gone," Randall said. "That ball of light is new."

The figure pointed down at the glowing ball, which then began to descend slowly on its way toward Earth. It moved with a steady decline until it vanished into the atmosphere. Its brightness intensified as it neared the surface.

FROM THE DEPTHS OF SPACE

Another giant flash emerged, and the Earth glowed in an amber hue.

Fires formed all across the Earth's surface. The bright glow disappeared into the planet while the flames intensified. The unnatural glow along the Earth spread further, crossing one another until the planet was illuminating orange from the blaze.

Macy shrieked in horror, breaking the silence and the breadth of emotions they'd all been holding back.

"No! No!" Randall yelled.

"This can't be real. This can't be real," Gunther repeated.

Randall looked to his crew, all of their expressions reflecting the horror he felt. Carter stared, in silence, as the planet burned. Randall struggled to comprehend the loss from so many decimated towns. He imagined the screams, the explosions, all the horrific loss playing in his head like a disaster film.

The figure hovered higher as the scorched planet burned. And then Randall locked eyes with it when it glanced up at their ship.

What are you? Randall thought.

"I am the one who will end it all."

The figure appeared in front of the main window. It had lanky limbs and a pastel purple skin. Its bone structure resembled that of humans, but its ability to breathe in space and its black eyes indicated to Randall that its body had already surpassed humanity's capabilities.

Everyone froze as it stared back at them curiously. Locking eyes with Randall again, the figure stretched its long arms to grip the ship outside the view from the main window. And when it spoke again, it was clear they all heard its words.

"I am the one who will end human existence."

The figure pushed at the ship, and the crew stumbled as the *Sempiternal* soared into the deepest reaches of space, beyond what any human had seen.

Randall and Macy held on to the support beams under a nearby table. Gunther gripped the legs of the control board. Carter braced himself against the corner of the main window, keeping his gaze trained on the figure as the vessel pushed deeper and deeper into blackness.

"What do you mean 'end all existence'?" Carter asked.

"I have capabilities beyond what lives now. I won't share it with a weaker race."

"You attacked our home without knowing our capabilities. Killing you is still possible within this ship," Carter said, looking at the controls.

Without hesitation, Carter swung up to the control panel. He scanned a board the size of a classroom chalkboard. That didn't stop him from finding the BACKUP THRUSTERS button and hammering his fist on it. The *Sempiternal* began to slow. Designed to aid in case the ship's main thrusters failed in deep space, the backups could give them a powerful jump toward a nearby moon or planet.

"Keep a tight grip, everyone," Carter said. "I'm blowing this asshole back into space."

Carter plugged the navigator's route back to their shattered home. The ship slid to an abrupt stop and knocked their assailant back. Carter dialed the speed up to full and shot forward, striking the figure and sending it rattling off the hull of the vessel.

"Where did it go?" Gunther asked, jumping to his feet and running to Carter.

"Get me eyes on the rear now," Carted demanded.

With several taps, the rearview camera displayed the figure floating behind the ship on the small display. The figure slowly raised its arms, as if reaching for the thrusters it coincidentally hovered between.

They all moved closer to watch.

"Hold on tight," Carter said, shooting the *Sempiternal* toward their former location.

Flames emerged from the thrusters, consuming the figure on the screen. Its body went instantly limp, floating like debris into the depths of space as their vessel sped toward their desired location.

Carter let out a sigh of relief. A second later he was working out calculations to prepare on how best to approach their damaged planet.

"That thing attacked our home. It's so horrible." Macy cried, dropping to her knees. "What if it comes back? What if it tries to destroy Earth?"

Randall kneeled to comfort Macy.

Carter brushed past them, momentarily glancing at her.

"I'll rip it in half with this ship if it survived that blast." He plugged away at the navigation. "We can circle back, but we need to assess the damage to the ship before I fire up the thrusters again. Come with me, Gunther."

"Carter, you did a great job saving us. Next time, don't risk the thrusters when we don't know where we are," Randall said.

"Sorry, Cap. I was a little busy to follow protocol," Carter said. "Besides, you were barely hanging on that table across the room. I had to act fast."

Randall approached Carter quickly, getting in his face. But Carter didn't even flinch, clearly not intimidated by Randall physically. But surely he knew he'd be demoted if Randall told the right people what he had done.

"Next time, ask," Randall said. "I don't need you risking our lives because you miss being a reckless pilot."

Randall walked back to Macy and helped her up, and they exited the room together, leaving Carter standing there watching them.

Gunther and Carter rushed to the back of the ship to evaluate the damage to the thrusters.

"I would've done the same thing," Gunther said. "Luckily, there doesn't appear to be much damage. We need to manually open one of the thrusters from the outside. I think that thing lost a hand there." Gunther kept his eyes on the controls.

"I've got twice the flight experience as that asshole and somehow I'm still his errand boy." Carter scoffed. "Fucking absurd." He reached for a spacesuit and started to put it on, gazing out the window after securing the tether and noticing some sort of burnt purple sludge coating the ship. "I ripped the fuck out of that thing, didn't I?"

"Sure did. Unless that thing can regenerate its one giant glob of space slime." Gunther chuckled.

Amused by his own achievement, Carter climbed into the airlock and closed the door behind himself. "Can you hear me okay in this thing?"

"Loud and clear, sir," Gunther said. He sealed the door to the ship and typed in the code, initiating the process that would open the outer hatch. "Ready when you are."

"Open it up." Carter waited for the doors to open completely before stepping out into the black void. He gazed at the distant planets and stars for a moment and then proceeded toward the locked thruster. "I'm on it. How bad is it?"

"Just jammed. I'm guessing more monster sludge. Scoop it out and I'll see if I can do a manual open," Gunther said.

"Make sure it's off. I don't want to add any sludge to this mess," Carter said.

When he got there, he reached in and pulled out some of that purple slime coating the inside of the thruster. It drifted into space. He pulled out more large globs, sending them on their way as well. Apart from some minor scrapes, the opening appeared clear.

Carter hovered to the side of the ship, making sure his tether was clear of the thruster.

"Okay, give it a try," he said.

"Testing now. Stay clear," Gunther said.

The thruster powered on and a blue glow emerged. It erupted with a blue flame and stabilized for several seconds.

Gunther, easily amused by small achievements, cheered. "Yes! Ready for action!"

"Are you clapping?" Carter asked.

"Hey, this kept us from being stranded out here. Let me have it," Gunther said. "I'm bringing you back in."

He heard Gunther tapping on keys, then he quieted. The controls went dead. Everything's gone black. "What happened?"

"Stop fucking around. Open the door so I can come back inside," Carter said. The lack of response made him impatient. "Gunther, you there?"

'No one else can hear us. We are alone now.'

Chills shot down Carter's spine. He turned his head and there was the being he thought had been decimated by the blast, now just a few dozen feet away from him.

"What? I killed you," Carter said.

The being extended its damaged arm. Within seconds, a stream of purple muscles intertwined, extending further. The being looked down, stretching its newly formed arm and flexing. Then it launched itself forward, stopping inches away from Carter.

"Holy shit. What do you want?"

'You are the alpha.'

"I'm not in charge. I just do what I think is best," Carter said.

'That was not a question. You are the alpha. A failed attempt to take my power, but still an admirable try.'

"Are you here to kill me?" Carter asked.

'Quite the opposite. I believe you can help me. Your home planet. Get me there.'

"Why would I? You probably destroyed a few cities with your little show back there," Carter said.

'I told you. I will be the one to end existence.'

"I'm not helping you destroy my home. I'd be stuck on this ship for the rest of my life," Carter said. "Besides, I don't even know why you think you could talk me into something like that. I am your enemy."

'You are my equal. We will end it together.'

The being placed both hands on Carter's helmet. A surge of electricity rushed through his body. Unable to move, Carter's eyes rolled back into his head, and he went numb. Inside his mind, he saw a blur of worlds exploding by his own hand. Carter was beside the purple being, hovering over the obliterated planets side by side. And he could breathe in the nothingness of space.

In this vision, he turned to the purple being, smiling. "On to the next planet."

His eyes beamed with joy, a reflection of the fiery decimated planet below.

His mind quickly returned to the present.

The being released its grip, tiny bolts of electricity bouncing around each finger as he withdrew them. Carter was more curious than afraid in that moment, realizing that he too had those same tiny bolts. As if by instinct, he pointed a finger randomly and fired a large bolt into the black depths of space.

He looked at his former rival, shocked.

'Now the power is yours to aid me. Do with it as you wish.'

The being shot back into space. The lights on the *Sempiternal* turned back on. A faint hum echoed from the ship as the outer lights illuminated and the power allowed the crew to return to their previous tasks, not to mention breathe without any sort of oxygen tank.

"Carter? You there? Lost you there for a bit," Gunther said over the radio. "We lost power and had to hurry to get into suits so we could breathe. The entire ship went dead."

"Yeah, still here."

"What the hell was that?"

"No clue," Carter said, lying.

"We've never had a power failure like that. Randall wants me to reel you back in before it happens again," Gunther said.

Carter's tether pulled slightly. He aimed for the outer door and pushed off the ship toward it. He slid inside, stabilizing while the airlock temporarily blocked him from the crew. Then he removed his space suit, noticing he was trembling. He felt some unnerving presence—whether from one of the crew members or the being itself, he couldn't tell.

'We can conquer together. Just get us back to your planet. I have found a way inside your vessel.'

The interior doors opened, and Gunther stood in the doorway, which startled Carter since he'd been lost in his mind.

"Glad to have you back, bud." Gunther smiled.

Gunther's constant perky attitude tended to annoy Carter. He often wondered if Gunther ever got mad or if anything bothered him.

Gunther thumbed toward the helm.

Carter rolled his eyes.

"Yeah, yeah. Let's get this meeting over with."

●

Gunther approached the helm while Carter peered down several hallways. He was nervous and didn't want to reveal his secret to the others. But he had to put on his game face, so he suppressed his fears and followed closely behind Gunther.

They turned the corner and there stood Randall.

"Are you both okay?" he asked.

"We're just dandy, Cap," Carter said sarcastically.

Randall shot Carter an annoyed look.

"No harm done, chief," Gunther said happily.

Carter couldn't resist another eye roll.

"Good to hear. Any idea what caused the power outage?" Randall asked.

"Not sure," Gunther said. "Maybe that creature had some sort of EMP effect on the ship. Otherwise, I'm out of ideas. I'm running diagnostics checks as we speak. Carter fixed the thruster so we should be back up and running in no time as long as there aren't any more problems."

"Perfect. Macy and I are going to figure out the course back to Earth. You two focus on the diagnostics, and we will check back in about an hour," Randall said.

"Copy," Carter said. He started away.

Macy grabbed his hand.

"Thank you. That could've been a lot worse," she said.

Carter stared at her, but his mind was focused on the purple figure. "Don't mention it."

Randall watched Gunther and Carter exit. He'd detected a shift in Carter's body language. Of course, he remained his normal wise ass self, but something felt off. They'd locked eyes, and what he'd seen in Carter's eyes had been fear.

He returned to the controls and punched in coordinates.

Macy paced the room slowly.

"I have no idea how far off course we are. I don't know if we need a week's worth of fuel or a month's," Randall said, sighing. Macy looked distressed. "What's wrong?"

"I have a weird feeling about Carter. He seemed...disturbed. Something was off."

Randall chuckled. "I see you finally boarded the ship."

"No, I'm serious. He had this look in his eyes… Something scared him, but I can't imagine what," Macy said.

Randall had seen that same look. "He was outside the ship when the power outage occurred. Maybe he got nervous being stuck out there," Randall said. "There aren't many things that could spook a guy like Carter."

"Maybe you're right. It still feels odd. Let's keep an eye on him."

"Let's figure out how to get home and then I'll take him to a spa when we land." Randall gave Macy a smile.

Macy and Randall punched in the coordinates.

Gunther ran the control board while Carter sat in the chair in the corner of the room. Carter saw Gunther glance over.

"How are you doing, big guy? You don't look so hot."

"I'm fine. How's the ship?" Carter asked.

"Seems fine to me. No problems came up in the diagnostics. I'm running it one more time, but I think it's just overkill. Either we had a one in a million chance of a power outage or that thing back there had powers beyond what we saw. Either way, we recovered well."

"What if it survived? Maybe it could follow us home if it can exist in outer space without needing oxygen."

"Considering it didn't just go right to the surface, maybe it's not capable of breaching our atmosphere. Besides, you made that freak into space slime, so we don't have anything to worry about anymore," Gunther said. He smiled and turned back to the controls.

"What if it didn't die? What if it boarded the ship when we thought it drifted off into space?" Carter asked.

"Do you really think it survived? It took a direct blast from the thrusters. You scraped its insides out of the thrusters. I seriously doubt even a highly advanced species could handle a hit like that. I think you're a bit spooked, and I don't blame you. We all are. Let's figure out the ship first and we can swap ideas on aliens afterward."

Carter stood and walked over to Gunther. Gunther backed away.

"You sure you're okay?" Gunther asked.

"Couldn't be better," Carter said. "Although, I have this neat new trick to show you. I learned it outside."

"What are you talking about?" Gunther asked.

Carter pointed toward a metal chair. "Watch, it's going to blow your mind."

A bolt of electricity shot across the room and lit up the chair. The bolt bounced around, illuminating the room in a bright white glow. Carter held the bolt for nearly thirty seconds before lowering his finger. The room remained silent, Gunther's jaw dropping open before curling into a smile.

"What? How? Can you—? Does Randall know?" Gunther said.

Carter grabbed Gunther and threw a hand over his mouth.

"Shut the fuck up. I just found out a little while ago. I saw that thing again outside. I think it did this to me." Carter pulled his hand away.

"Wait… Did you talk to it?" Gunther gripped his own hair, tugging as if in disbelief. He backed away, seeming both curious and scared of Carter's newfound ability.

"It spoke to me. It talked inside my head, as it didn't have a mouth," Carter said. The purple figure flashed in his thoughts.

'I hope you know what you are doing by telling him this information. Do not delay our mission.'

"It has telepathy? That's wild! We should tell Randall and Macy about your find." Gunther headed for the door.

Carter blocked Gunther before he could exit, gripping Gunther's shoulder. "No. This is between us. I don't want them knowing."

"Why not?" Gunther asked.

Carter still hadn't processed his encounter. It barely made sense to him. He hadn't thought it out entirely and could feel the pressure from this lingering presence on the ship. A creak from the ship could mean it was scratching around somewhere. Ringing from the controls could've meant it opened the doors to the outside and they were seconds away from being sucked into space.

'Is he our ally or our enemy?'

The purple figure stood at the end of the hallway. It gazed at Carter and pointed to his hands.

Carter saw the bolts bouncing between his fingertips. He released his grip from Gunther and when he glanced back down the hallway, the figure was gone.

"Ally," Carter said.

"What did you say?" Gunther asked.

"Whatever that thing is, whatever it did to me,

it knows I want something more than to be Randall's errand boy. It will do the same for you too. We can be powerful beings on Earth. Beings to be worshiped and praised for our efforts," Carter said.

"By doing what? What makes you think I want to be a part of that?" Gunther asked.

Carter extended both hands. Large bolts shot toward the ceiling and bounced around the room. "Because of this. We can do this. We can have all the power we want."

"You're scaring me, man. If you don't tell Randall about this, I will." Gunther attempted to step past him, but he tripped on Carter's foot and fell to the ground.

"What the hell is wrong with you?"

"I was wrong. He's an enemy," Carter said. He lunged at Gunther and wrapped his hands around Gunther's neck.

'Show him how we deal with enemies.'

Carter dug his nails into Gunther's throat and released several bolts. Gunther's body shook with severity and his eyes bulged from his head. Foam leaked from the sides of his mouth, and he groaned as words failed to form.

Carter squeezed harder, the smell of burning flesh overwhelming him. Black marks formed on Gunther's face. The whites of his eyes erupted and started to smoke. Gunther continued to kick his legs despite taking so much electricity directly to his neck and head.

Carter released his grip to catch his breath.

'Keep going.'

Gunther struggled to move, his fried body too weak and even when he attempted to form words, he failed.

Carter just stared.

'You aren't done. Keep going.'

"He's going to die. I don't need to do anything else. If I do more, the others might hear," Carter said.

The figure appeared behind him. It squeezed Carter's shoulder, forcing him to kneel and whimper in pain.

'I gave you this power to use it for my benefit. You, humans, are weak, but your will is admirable. Finish what you started so I may complete my journey to the surface.'

Carter reached down and squeezed both sides of Gunther's head and unleashed more current. Blood poured from Gunther's eyes, soaking Carter's hands. It took more than thirty seconds for Gunther to stop moving and by then the room was permeated with the smell of burnt flesh.

Carter stared into Gunther's lifeless, blackened eyes.

'The first of many. Time to get this ship back to your planet.'

The figure disappeared, and Carter was left with the first dead body he was responsible for.

He hadn't realized the ship had started moving while displaying his new power. Randall and Macy had reactivated the thrusters and put them back on course toward Earth.

He quietly made his way to the front of the ship, listening in on Randall and Macy's conversation before making his presence known in case they'd heard the confrontation.

"They're taking an awfully long time back there," Macy said. "Obviously the ship is functioning all right. What else could they be running diagnostics for?"

"Gunther probably has Carter cornered in another science fiction hypothesis. After all, we did witness alien life. I'm sure Carter wants to blow his brains out right now," Randall said.

Macy chuckled. "That or Carter already strangled him and is throwing his corpse out into space."

"You guys have no faith in me at all. I'd be much more violent when it came to Gunther's death," Carter said.

Macy visibly jumped in surprise.

Randall faced the door, looked Carter up and down, then shot Macy a glance. Carter walked to the corner of the room and sat down.

Randall put some distance in between himself and Macy as he approached Carter.

"Is everything okay back there? Where's Gunther?"

"Has his face buried in the controls. I wanted to get some peace and quiet for a moment," Carter said. He wasn't lying, either. Carter had made sure Gunther was resting in the chair before he went to the head of the ship. Gunther's burnt face wouldn't be visible upon first glance if someone had walked past the rear control room.

"You're not assisting him?" Randall asked.

"He said he had it under control, so I came up here. Is that a problem?" Carter flexed his fingers and cracked each knuckle repeatedly.

Randall walked back toward the controls and eyed Macy. Carter knew they both distrusted him. The way Macy and Randall constantly shot glaring stares at each other solidified to him that they were growing fearful of the situation.

Macy walked to Carter.

"What was the diagnosis?"

Carter kept his head down, ignoring her question. He didn't think for one second that they'd believe Gunther was fine in the back. The tension building in the room started to rattle Carter's nerves. He still tried to play it cool.

"I see you guys got the ship moving. What's our timeline?" Carter asked.

"Timeline?" Macy asked.

"Yeah. How long until we get home?"

"We aren't entirely sure. Neither of us can figure out how far we were blasted into space. Fortunately, we can still track coms from Earth, so we plotted a course. It could be an hour, or it could be a month," Randall said.

"We're going to run out of fuel in under a month. What's the plan then?" Carter asked.

"Well, we wanted to discuss that with you and Gunther. We have enough for one skip. If everyone is okay with it, we can do it and get home in about a day," Randall said. "Why don't you go get Gunther and we can discuss it?"

"I already told you, he's busy in the back. I'm sure he's fine with it," Carter said.

"I'd be more comfortable with him here. I'll go get him," Randall said.

Carter stepped in the way, blocking Randall.

"Carter, please get out of the way."

Randall and Carter stared at each other silently. Carter had never displayed rebellion like this before outside of an argument about what was necessary as far as maintenance for the ship. He would argue for hours about why mopping the floor could be a weekly task instead of every other day, but he'd always back down eventually. Now though, he stood his ground.

'I can hear your leader's heart pounding. He fears you.'

Carter didn't budge.

Randall stepped slightly closer. "Carter, this stare down alone could get you in trouble. It's best to be wise about your next move. I don't want to demote you, but I'll make damn sure it happens."

"Come on, Carter," Macy said. "There's no need to be a hothead about this. Ego aside, Randall is still in charge. Just take a step back and we can all be civil." If she had been scared before, it escalated by this point.

Carter had refused to break eye contact with Randall, but now he looked over at Macy and smiled at her. He took a step back so Randall could have a clear path to the back. Carter chuckled as Randall hesitated, which quickly devolved laughing hysterically. He gave Randall a hard pat on the back.

"Man, I definitely had you convinced for a minute there! Your eyes bugged out of your head!" Carter exclaimed. "Go on, go get your super genius."

Randall smirked and exhaled deeply. "You asshole. You really had me there." He walked past Carter and shot Macy another glance. Their frequent shared expressions was starting to piss Carter off.

Macy smiled at Carter when they exchanged looks.

Randall had no idea what Carter had planned.

"I really should save you the time though," Carter said. "I killed Gunther about a half-hour ago. I'm taking over this ship, and there's nothing you can do to stop me."

Macy and Randall shared a look of terror.

"Gunther's dead?" Macy asked. "No, this is just another one of your sick jokes."

"I wouldn't joke about something like this. I killed him with my new powers, and I'll do the same to both of you if you try to stop me," Carter said.

"You're bluffing. None of this is funny anymore," Randall said. He stepped toward Carter and grabbed him by the shoulder.

"I have no need to bluff. I can kill you, too," Carter said. He extended his fingers, launching bright bolts into the ceiling. Carter threw a punch into Randall's chest, launching him into the wall and Randall's head smacked into it, knocking him unconscious as he collapsed to the floor.

"Randall," Macy screamed.

Carter glared at her. Macy ran back to the adjacent hallway, barely missing the bolts Carter threw her direction. Macy had gotten down the hall quickly.

Carter walked over to Randall's body. The purple figure appeared next to him.

'Is he deceased?'

"Not yet. I need him alive for the time being," Carter said.

'And his spouse? She has escaped.'

"I know where she's going. It's all part of the plan. We are at a standstill until we are in Earth's reach," Carter said.

'If I got you there faster, could it escalate our timeline?'

"Of course. Tell me when you're ready. I'll deal with her," Carter said.

The figure walked off to the back of the ship. Carter rushed toward the hallway Macy had escaped through.

Macy thought it was a prank Gunther had come up with. Gunther didn't have the dark sense of humor Carter did, but he often laughed at Carter's jokes. When Macy saw Gunther's burnt face resting on the control panel, she broke down in tears. She had watched Randall take a hard blow and she wasn't sure he'd recover. Now, she was the last one standing against Carter.

Panicking, Macy looked around for something to defend herself with. They were a research team that had been sent out to study and test new gear for advanced space travel, so there wasn't much for her to fight a recently enhanced human. The *Sempiternal* was essentially a laboratory capable of going as far as the outer moons of Jupiter. This knowledge was limited to the crew and certain members of the space program, so most of the civilians had no idea. All Macy had available was a nonconducting space suit that would maybe shield her from the bolts of electricity.

Putting it on as quickly as possible, she heard footsteps.

"Do you know why I admire you so much, Macy?" Carter asked. "It's because I could tell you saw a change before anyone got hurt. Your senses are better than I give you credit for."

"Is that something I'm supposed to be proud of? What you're doing is insane and it won't end well for you" Macy said.

Carter extended his hands and flexed while the bolts shot across the room. They bounced from beam to beam, around the control board, and across the ceiling.

"Once I touch down on Earth, I will be superior to everyone in charge. No more bad marks. No more petty commands. And no more waiting around for someone else to make a difference. I can take over. We will rule over everyone! They'll bow to our orders!" Carter said as he extended his arms in the air, firing more bolts across the room.

"We? Who is the other part of that?" Macy asked.

"It's on the ship, Macy. I thought it was our enemy, but it isn't. It granted me this power, and I'll make sure it gets what it wants," Carter said.

The purple figure entered the room and stood behind Carter. It glared at Macy, and she backed away while trying to find the nearest escape. The side entrance was close enough for her to make a run for it. She contemplated doing just that, maybe find a place to hide or go see if Randall was still alive.

Macy slid her foot and shifted her body toward the side entrance. She looked in the direction and froze.

'I will catch you before you reach the entrance.'

It's in my head! It knows what I'm going to do, Macy thought.

"Don't do it, Macy," Carter said. "Make this easy on yourself. Get us back to Earth and do it quickly. We will handle it from there."

"Of course. You got it, Carter," Macy said.

Macy's stare shifted immediately from Carter to the door. She turned and moved her back leg, shifting it toward the side entrance. She had no other choice but to try. She wasn't going to wait to die by Carter's hands. She wanted to check on Randall and hide.

She made it within a foot's reach of the door and then the figure appeared in front of her, extending its massive arms, blocking any escape.

'You will not escape. Do not fight what we command.'

Macy couldn't pass him and noticed Carter approaching her. He stood behind her for a moment before wrapping his arms around her neck. "Why don't we get this off of you, so you know what the current feels like."

None of them noticed the person stepping into the doorway behind the behemoth alien. As he lifted the steel bar, Macy saw Randall coming up behind this giant creature and prepare to fight if needed.

'Do not fight us.'

As Macy heard those words in her head, the bar came down and crashed into the creature's head. Purple sludge erupted from the wound, which Macy believed was blood. It splattered across the room, drenching Carter's hands and chest.

Macy saw a toolbox on the table beside her and opened it.

The creature dropped to the floor, and Carter went after Randall. Macy took a moment to dig through the toolbox and found a wrench, which she threw at

Carter's face. He screamed when it hit, a rapid flow of blood dripping from his nose as a result of the blow.

"That's definitely a broken nose," Macy said, smiling at Randall.

"I'll kill you first, you fucking bitch," Carter said.

He charged Macy. The steel bar came down again before he got too far and struck him in the temple. Carter stumbled then collapsed into a shelf, falling backward and toppling the contents down on top of him. The large load buried him underneath.

Randall reached for Macy and pulled her close.

"Come on. We have a way out of here. We need to be quick if it's going to work," Randall said.

"Way out of here? What are you talking about?" Macy asked.

"I'll explain when we're away from these freaks."

Macy followed Randall to the front of the ship, hopeful now that she knew there was a way to escape Carter and his newfound friend once and for all.

Macy and Randall entered the main control room. Randall took a break to catch his breath. After taking such a hard hit, he wasn't fully recovered, especially after fighting off both Carter and that being.

He lunged at Macy and kissed her.

"We brought a satellite up to test its capabilities of possibly landing as well as orbiting," Randall said. "It can land on a planet or moon as long as it has the coordinates and it's within range of the atmosphere. Carter doesn't know, but I had Gunther fix it in his spare time. If we can get in it when we're close enough to Earth, we can leave them stranded here."

"The skip. We can still make the jump while they're down. Leave Carter behind to fend for himself," Macy said.

"We make the jump, launch the satellite, and we're home free," Randall said.

"That thing can survive outside of the ship. What are we going to do about that?" Macy asked.

"We can leave them floating back into space. I'll schedule a reroute once we get into the satellite."

"Be quick. We have no idea when one of them could wake up," Macy said.

Randall handed Macy a walkie talkie. "I'll be with you the whole time. I love you."

Macy kissed Randall. He ran down the hall and disappeared into a corridor. She didn't know at that moment if she would ever see him again.

Macy locked in on the controls, hammering away at the coordinates she had for Earth. She programmed the skip in and gripped the throttle then hesitated. Throwing the ship forward made her nervous with two lethal foes only fifty feet away. More so, what was the plan if they were both dead? Randall and she would have to explain why they abandoned the *Sempiternal* and left three dead bodies on board.

She pulled her walkie talkie up to her face.

"Randall. Are we jumping into this too quickly? We should make sure they're dead or contained before we move on. An unguarded attack could ruin our escape."

She gripped the throttle while she awaited the response. Her gut told her to go ahead with the skip and save herself the short timeline that might allow Carter or that creature to wake up. Her conscience told her it could end Randall's life if she went too soon, and then she would be trapped with both their enemies and all alone. All the awful things they could do to her bounced around in her mind.

Static was the only answer she received. She stared at the walkie and awaited Randall's voice. Seconds felt like minutes. She let go of the throttle and gripped the walkie with both hands, skeptical that Randall could even answer as he approached the loading bay where the satellite rested.

"Randall, come on. Can you hear me?" Macy asked.

A small pile of hard plastic and wires landed at Macy's feet. It was Randall's walkie talkie. She saw the creature standing in the doorway, holding Randall up with its arm through his stomach. Macy dropped her walkie talkie, watching in horror as the creature stepped forward. The creature dropped Randall at her feet.

Carter came up beside the creature, flexing his electric power.

"Two down. Think we can finish you before we get back to Earth?"

'If you aid us, no harm will come to you.'

Macy peered over at the main window as an idea brewed in her mind. She could run; they'd find her. She could fight back, and they'd kill her. But she could go along with their plan and stop them when they least expected it. It was worth a try.

She looked Carter in the eye.

"So, what's next? Kill me? You can't fly this ship on your own. At least let me get us back to the atmosphere." Macy raised her chin proudly, thinking she had outsmarted Carter. "As for this thing, I know you're capable of finishing me off rather quickly, but it'll make no difference if neither of you can get this ship back to Earth."

"The skip. Do it," Carter demanded.

Macy sat in the seat in front of the controls and grabbed the throttle. She pushed it forward, launching them forward. The creature planted its feet, stabilizing itself. Carter held on to a nearby support bar. Darkness overwhelmed their view, the distant stars offering little relief for the surrounding vastness of space. Within a minute, a steady beep alerted Macy of their proximity to Earth. She pulled the throttle back.

The *Sempiternal* slowed to a stop not far from their location prior to the violent encounter. She let go of the controls and looked down at her home, unsure if she would ever step foot there again. She remembered her last memory with Randall, sitting at their favorite restaurant as the last patrons strolled in for the night, until the manager closed the doors and kicked everyone out. She soaked in the fond memory.

"It's always more beautiful from up here. I hate being down there sometimes," Carter said. He walked to Macy and placed his hand on her shoulder. "At least we will touch down there all the wiser, right?"

"Funny. You were never wise before. What makes you think you are now?" Macy said.

Carter chuckled and walked to the window. He nodded at the creature, inviting it over with him. It walked over to Carter, standing beside him. They shared a glance at Earth, peering at what would soon be theirs.

Macy looked across the control board, finding an immediate solution that could buy her some time.

"What will you do first?" Carter asked.

'Let the world know I am among them.'

"How will you do that?" Carter asked. "There are billions of people and you have so many places to start."

'I let your team know through conflict. I will cause greater conflict down there.'

Macy saw her opportunity. Enough fuel for another skip. They were distracted and celebrating what they considered a victory. Carter and the creature would never expect an attack from Macy. She knew if she failed it would lead to a swift and painful death. There was no certainty either of them would allow her to go free if they landed and docked. All she had left was her freedom, and even that was bleak at a time like this.

Macy plugged another skip into the controls. She held the throttle again, unsure if it was the right decision. Tears formed in her eyes, and she let out a whimper.

Carter noticed and faced her. He smiled at her tears then stepped forward and that's when he noticed her hand gripping the throttle. His smile widened.

"I'm pleased to see you are cooperating. I assure you we will make this easy on you when we reach the surface."

Macy looked back at Randall's stiff body. Hey eyes softened on him before shooting back to Carter with a glare. She squeezed the throttle and turned the directional dial, aiming at the blackness of space.

"Randall would want me to do the right thing." Macy threw the throttle forward, launching them into another skip.

Carter fell to the ground and the creature flew forward, cracking the main window. Macy rejoiced in the fact that she would ruin their plans. She glanced down and saw the fuel gauge depleting as she continued to push the *Sempiternal* into the void.

'You must stop her.'

Carter stood, bracing himself on a table behind Macy, pointing his hands at her. "Don't do this, Macy.

You can make it to the end of this alive!"

"I'd rather be dead, Carter. Do what you have to," Macy said as she stared down at the fuel gauge, watching it drain further.

The creature stood and glared at Carter.

'Stop her or everything is ruined for us both.'

Carter flexed his fingers, shooting a light jolt into Macy. She flinched but pushed the throttle up as far as it would reach. With each threatening shock, Macy stood her ground.

The creature walked toward Carter. He looked back, seeming unsure if the creature was pursuing him or Macy.

"We will kill you, Macy. Don't you dare think I won't do it myself," Carter yelled.

He shot a longer bolt at her. It radiated up her spine. She gripped the controls tighter. But Macy was determined to strand them as far away as she could before she released her grip. She clenched her teeth and fought back the urge to scream and pressed on.

Carter broke concentration to look up at the creature, angrily staring back at him. The creature flexed his own hand and the bolts from Carter's fingers stopped abruptly. They locked eyes momentarily. Larger bolts erupted from Carter's fingers, not only shooting into Macy but bouncing across the room.

Macy screamed but maintained her grip.

'You must take back your control.'

"I'm trying," Carter yelled.

'Try harder. Make her break or I will!'

"You're going to kill us, you asshole," Carter yelled.

The creature struck Carter, knocking him into the wall. A loud snap echoed through the room and Carter slumped to the ground, gripping his arm firmly. The creature was now standing behind Macy but staring at him.

'I gave you power beyond what you'll ever conceive. I'll show you how to use it.'

Macy regained her composure now that the bolts had stopped assaulting her. The fuel gauge was about to breach the red zone and put them in a critical point of no return. She exhaled as the monitor in front of her went black. She saw the reflection of the creature winding back to swing at her and ducked. The full force of the blow went straight into the monitor, glass embedding in the creature's wrist, causing purple sludge to leak out into the control panel.

Macy fell back into the workstation, feeling around its surface. Her knuckles grazed a large wrench and she gripped it firmly.

'I can survive in space. You two have only delayed my mission.'

"You won't get off this ship though," Macy said as she swung the tool at the creature's skull, landing the blow and splattering more sludge on the floor.

She swung repeatedly, making the sludge on the floor form a small pool at the creature's feet. When she brought it down again, the creature grabbed her hand and tore the wrench free of her hand, then tossed it across the room. But Macy had found another tool and brought it around with just as much force, each blow making the small pool larger. The creature didn't seem to notice the gaping wound in its head.

"Carter! Carter, get up and help me." Macy yelled. She didn't hear a response and barely glanced over to see if he had any fight left in him or if he was even alive for that matter.

'He's dead. You will be soon as well.'

The creature swung its head down and connected with the bridge of Macy's nose. She stumbled back, blood immediately dripping down her face. She caught herself against the wall and wiped the blood from her face. She gripped the closest thing she could find and ran at the creature, ready to fight with everything she had left.

A steel beam ripped through the creature's face before she got there, exploding out of its cheek from the back of its head. Purple sludge dripped down its neck. Carter appeared behind it and jumped up onto the controls. He gripped a beam tightly and pulled the creature toward him, turning its head to face Macy.

Carter nodded at Macy.

"It's how it has to be. We all go. I'm sorry about Randall."

There was hardly enough time for Macy to react before the glowing light from Carter's hands shined brightly throughout the room. Macy covered her eyes and heard Carter scream. The bolts scattered across the control board while maintaining a steady current through the creature's head. Carter gritted his teeth, fighting the pain he caused himself. The creature's flesh bubbled and leaked out more purple sludge.

It reached its hand up to grip Carter's neck.

'*I... gave you...this power.*'

"We are both...going to die...because of it," Carter screamed out.

The creature squeezed Carter's neck. Carter tried to free himself of the grip, but it made no difference. Carter swayed back and forth but maintained pressure on the creature's wrist. The creature tugged at its wrist until it abruptly slid out of the shattered monitor. Swinging his arm down again, Carter lost grip on the steel bar and the current stopped. Carter fell to the floor, scrambling in the pool of purple sludge.

The creature flexed its fist. Glass shards dropped from its skin.

It reached down, pulling Carter up by his neck. Carter gripped its arm, still trying to kill it with more current. The creature's purple flesh bubbled, the sludge now leaking out with more severity. But the creature seemed fine despite the grotesque flesh, its lack of pain obvious, the matter seeming trivial as it squeezed Carter's neck. It swung its now free arm up and struck Carter in the face several times. Blood poured from Carter's eye and nose as the skin on his face opened further with each blow.

Finally, Carter's grip loosened, and he went limp.

'It was my error to assume you were worthy.'

The creature reached back to strike Carter, and that's when the ship's controls and interior lights went black then flickered back on briefly, then off again. The ship slowed to a steady rotation and grew darker by the second. The creature lowered Carter, taking in the view through the *Sempiternal's* viewscreen.

Carter grinned.

"Macy, where are we?"

She stood at the broken controls, keeping the tool she'd wielded handy. "The same black hole this asshole came from. It's where we will all die."

'I won't die among the likes of you.'

Carter swung one hand at the creature, poking his fingers into its eye and forced his forearm as deep as into its head possible. Then he let the power surge from his hand, placing his other hand on the side of the creature's face. He fought the creature as it squirmed about, trying to shake him, but continued his assault to overpower it.

The creature leaked more sludge, drenching Carter's arms. It dropped to its knees and its arms dangled as Carter held it up with the powerful current erupting from his hands. The bubbling flesh gave way and the creature's head exploded, soaking the walls and Carter and even Macy.

The lifeless alien dropped to the ground.

Carter fell back, breathing heavily as the strength left him. His arms remained outstretched, resting from his difficult battle. He looked over at Macy, who approached him, still holding the tool she'd found.

"No sense doing anything foolish at this point. We're lying on our deathbeds. Let's just enjoy the borrowed time," Carter said.

Macy walked over to the main window and gazed out, imagining that she saw Earth. The illusion faded into blackness. She smiled at Carter.

"It's funny. I knew exactly what and where I was going to be with Randall a week from now. There's this tiny restaurant a few blocks from our home. It's where he proposed. I rented out the entire restaurant for one night as a surprise for him," Macy said. "You're right, though. No sense in letting it upset me. There's no sense of anything, anymore."

Crack!

The main window's glass further cracked as Macy swung her tool into it again and again with all her strength.

"What the fuck are you doing?" Carter yelled. "You're going to kill us."

"I already have. I'm making the countdown shorter," Macy said as she continued to swing the tool against the glass. What started as a small crack grew to spiderweb. She continued to swing. The center of the window, which now looked like a snowball, maintained and it surprised Macy how durable it was after such abuse.

"Macy. We can send a distress signal. Think about this," Carter said.

Macy brought the tool back. "It's all I've been thinking about since I saw my husband die. You deserve this as badly as I want it!"

Macy swung the tool into the glass and the vacuum pulled through the small hole she created. It was a matter of seconds before the glass was torn into space, and Macy was sucked out into the black depth. Every loose item scattered around the room was ripped from their locations into the emptiness around her. Carter had held on, but he could see his air depleting. The opposite wall folded inward, crumbling toward him.

The last few moments of his life would be spent watching the *Sempiternal* crumble and fold into a mass of wires and bent steel. As the ship collapsed on him Carter was forced to let go and was sucked out into the darkness.

His skin developed frost immediately and each breath felt like inhaling a blizzard. He didn't see Macy, Randall, Gunther, or the creature tossed from the wreckage or floating about.

As this heartbeat slowed and his brain activity slowed, a faint bolt trickled out of Carter's fingertips. His body was further pulled hundreds of miles from the empty ship, the former crew, and the creature that had promised him a better life. The *Sempiternal* floated in one direction and Carter was pushed elsewhere, forgotten in space and all by his lonesome.

PIECING TOGETHER

The night sky glowed with electric blue. Soundless lightning lit up the dark sky, glowing above the men's BBQ night. Cliff, Omar, and Mitch stared on, biting into their second helping of burgers.

"Either of you know what this could be?" Cliff asked.

"Not a clue, buddy." Omar continued into his burger.

"Fuck if I know either. Just happy to be enjoying this grill finally." Mitch downed his second beer.

Cliff had his eyes on the sky when his phone rang. Alicia hardly ever called unless there was something wrong in her troubled relationship with Dennis. It must have been urgent.

"Alicia, how are you?" Cliff asked.

There was a pause, but her heavy breathing said everything. "Cliff, I don't know what your friend did, but you need to come check on him. I've had enough. If I don't get out of the house right now, I'm going to strangle him."

"What happened this time?"

Alicia wasn't a stranger to verbally assaulting Dennis in the front of the house for all the neighbors to see. Dennis, used to the cruelty his wife of nine years had dished out over time, took the words like jabs to the gut. Heavy, but he knew how to keep going afterward.

"I'm trying to get ready to go out and somehow, he broke the fucking kitchen window. When I asked him about it, he just babbled. He went down into the basement and still hasn't answered me. I'm done with him tonight. I don't know how much longer I can do this."

Cliff eyed Omar and Mitch, hinting with his expression that they needed to go over there.

Omar smiled and Mitch rolled his eyes.

Cliff stood, waving his comrades over. "Okay, we'll pack up some food and bring it over. No need to get worked up. Go have fun with the ladies. Talk to you soon."

Alicia hung up without so much as a sigh. Cliff was used to her bringing him into their marital problems, which Dennis was often quiet about, despite Cliff offering aid whenever needed.

"Well, guess I'll get to use these new bad boys a little longer." Cliff pointed at his running shoes. He couldn't help himself from talking about his running hobby. "Alicia wants us to check on Dennis. He was acting funny."

Mitch rolled his eyes again, letting out a loud sigh as he cracked open his third beer and stacked a few prepped burgers on a plate.

"So, Dennis isn't showing up? Christ, does she even let him out of the house when she's not there?"

"They're having marital problems. You wouldn't be thrilled about being with someone if your personal life wasn't going well."

"I'd bury my face in the first pair of stripper's tits that would have me," Mitch said, and smiled before sipping his beer.

Omar and Cliff had never been comfortable with Mitch's crudeness, but he had a great setup for guy's night. Taking advantage of their friend's home justified his behavior.

"Let's at least bring him a plate before the night's over," Omar said. "He could use some chow after the Alicia storm."

The blue lightning burst again. The color lit the sky, spreading blue fingers all over the darkness. Thunder didn't follow, so the men looked on in wonder.

"Can't be lightning. Solar flare, maybe?"

"Maybe it's bits of an asteroid burning up in the atmosphere," Omar said. "Must be."

Cliff shrugged.

Mitch hardly seemed phased by anything anymore. He took another sip of his beer.

"Are we going to Dennis' or are we going to stare at the stars like teenage girls?" he said.

The three men made their way down the road to Dennis'. It was a pretty quiet walk. Mitch commented on the questionable lawn decor in the Ross' yard, and Cliff kept discussing his frequent cardio exercises.

Omar took a burger from the full plate. "I need some protein. Pressed three fifty this morning," Omar said while flexing his leg-sized arms. He bit into the burger.

"Exactly what we need…A giant black guy to keep us in line," Mitch smiled. "Besides, we need the diversity points."

"Mitch, enough with the race comments." Cliff's eyes darted over to his friend, who allowed his drunken thoughts to regurgitate out of his mouth too often.

The sky radiated with the vibrant blue light again. This time it was brighter and flowed like blood in prominent varicose veins. It wasn't as sporadic as heat lighting, glowing in the sky for several seconds before vanishing again.

The sky flashed again, pulling the guys from their conversation.

Cliff stood and stared at them before looking back to the sky.

"Let me call Molly. She's good with astronomy." Cliff reached for his phone.

Mitch gripped his wrist before he could dial.

"Hello! Guys' night. Let the science teacher form a hypothesis once we get over there." Mitch bit down again into his food.

Cliff pondered if his appetite for BBQ would soak up his beers.

"Maybe you should join me for a run this week, Mitch. You could burn off some of that frustration," Cliff said while dialing Dennis' number.

"Yeah, only if I can get matching pink shoes."

Dennis' phone rang with no answer.

Omar was the first to see Dennis' house and noticed the smoke.

"Guys? Something's definitely wrong," he said.

Mitch and Cliff saw the smoke, too, pouring out of the broken kitchen window. Flickering flames were dim but present.

They ran to open the back door and saw the counter was on fire.

"Put that out. I'll find Dennis," Cliff said. He turned on the lights to the stairwell and quickly climbed up, searching the bedrooms.

Omar got enough water on the counter to put out the fire.

Mitch inspected the broken window.

"I don't know how this idiot burned out his window, but this stunt is going to get him even deeper in husband jail."

Omar slapped Mitch across the chest. "Not the time for fucking jokes. We need to make sure he's okay."

Cliff searched every room, only to find each one darker than the previous. His frequent calls were answered by further silence. He could hear the struggle between Mitch and Omar downstairs. The noise got louder, and more and more it sounded like a conflict was brewing between them.

"Guys, any luck down there?" Cliff asked.

"I'd get down here if I were you," Omar said.

Cliff descended the stairs and reentered the kitchen. He could see his friends' horrified faces and also heard some distant sound. *Where is that coming from, and what is it?*

It was barely an audible whisper.

"There." Omar pointed to the basement stairs.

Cliff leaned closer, hearing the sound clearer now that he knew where it came from.

Mitch gripped his holster, unclipping and drawing his pistol.

"What the fuck are you doing? You're not going to shoot Dennis," Omar said, grabbing Mitch's wrist.

Mitch pulled away and aimed his gun toward the stairs. He approached slowly. "Cliff, get the light."

"Mitch, don't. Wait and see what happens. I can handle him on my own, without the gun."

"What if someone broke in and killed Dennis? I want to take that fucker down. I could be a goddamn hero," Mitch said.

Omar stepped closer to the basement, getting ahead of Mitch. "Relax, Rambo."

The sound grew louder, and Cliff was further intrigued. The sound was so familiar to him. It sounded like Dennis' voice, but not the words he expected. He tried to ignore his friends' bickering, but they were making it impossible to hear anything.

"Both of you, quiet! Listen," he said.

A faint mantra echoed from the basement. Words, repeating over and over, coming from the depths of the house. The words mashed together in a monotonous repetition, with a single breath separating the sentences. Cliff tried to grasp what the sentence was. He peered down the stairs, only to stare into the blackness.

Cliff listened closer, and now he heard more clearly.

"I am one but will become whole," Dennis whispered softly from the lower floor.

Inhale.

"I am one but will become whole."

Inhale.

"I am one but will—"

Cliff's eyes met Dennis' when he looked up from the basement. A darkness, even visible within the dark basement, stared back at Cliff. Those weren't the eyes Cliff knew.

Feet stomped up the stairs, and Cliff shot back next to Omar and Mitch. Mitch pointed his gun at the stairs, the creaking and stomping sounds overpowering their heavy breathing. Dennis stood at the top step. Darkness still covered most of his head, like a cloud hovering over him.

Cliff stepped forward again.

"Not too close, Cliff. Something's wrong," Omar said. "I got this."

Dennis shifted, facing them. Omar approached slowly. "Dennis, you okay? What happened here?"

"I don't like this at all," Mitch said. "Hey, dickhead. What happened? Is he fucking mute? Hello? Dennis?"

Cliff slapped Mitch across the chest and said, "Hey, knock it off."

Dennis stepped into the light, exposing the crawling mass of blue that had consumed most of his head. His right eye glowed with a vibrant white light, and the blue mass had spread into the corner of his mouth, causing his teeth to become blindingly white.

Mitch cocked his gun. "Don't you fucking move or I'll open your ugly face."

"Whoa, slow down, Mitch. Dennis, what is this? What the hell do you have on your head?" Omar asked.

Cliff clicked his phone open and quickly dialed 911. "Hello, I'm at 424 Hillside Road. My friend is acting erratically and destroyed part of his house. I need an officer right—"

Dennis' tongue shot out of his mouth, a sharp edge snapping Cliff's phone in half and grazing his face. Both pieces of the phone fell to the ground, the edges sizzling from what appeared to be acidic saliva. Cliff rubbed his face trying to get the fluid off, because it was burning his skin.

"I got this, Cliff. No cop is going to do anything for us," Mitch said, stepping closer to Dennis.

Dennis looked at each one of them. The blue mass on his head had shifted to the top of his skull, clearing his face. He smiled, taking their breath away.

"I am one but will become whole," Dennis said.

"What the fuck does that mean?" Mitch asked.

Dennis' tongue sprung from his mouth again, splattering the gun with its burning fluid. Mitch squeezed the trigger twice, sending Dennis flying back toward the living room.

"Are you out of your fucking mind?" Omar wrapped his heavy arms around Mitch, pulling him to the ground. His muscular build quickly allowed him to overpower Mitch, who wouldn't release his grip on the gun. "You just killed your fucking friend, man!"

"That is not my friend. Something was in control of him. Let me the fuck go, asshole." Mitch slammed the butt of his gun into Omar's head several times, but to no avail. Omar's hulking build kept him in control.

Cliff started pulling Omar away from Mitch. Omar made no effort to fight Cliff, the most reasonable one of the group, but his disdain for Mitch was still apparent. Omar walked over to Dennis, who laid still.

The blue mass crawled across Dennis' face to the top of his head. Blood dripped from his chest and collarbone, forming a small puddle on the floor.

"Is this because of what happened at the store today? You need to be some hero?"

"What happened at the store today?" Cliff looked back and forth between his friends.

"Someone called him 'trailer trash' at the grocery store today." Omar was pointing at Mitch.

Mitch had become the laughing stock of the town after a few of his 'drunken episodes' had left his yard and made their way through town. Walking into the mini mart nude, vomiting in a teacher's yard, screaming his son's name in the middle school parking lot, and that was just within the last two weeks. Mitch had heard all of the whispers and went off when a few kids yelled 'trailer trash' down the aisle while he and Omar were shopping. Omar had chased the kids away before returning to comfort his friend. There was little discussion about it afterward, but the amount of beer bottles that had piled up beside Mitch earlier didn't convey that he'd been taking it well.

Mitch pointed his gun at Omar. "You shut the fuck up about that."

"Mitch, calm down." Cliff put his hand on the gun, pulling it from Mitch's grip. "Let's just figure everything out calmly."

"I would've beat those little fuckers if you hadn't chased them away. Next time they won't be so lucky."

Cliff pulled Mitch up. "You better hope you didn't kill him. Come on, let's wait for the cops."

●

The flashing lights were visible within minutes of Cliff walking outside. Two officers emerged from their squad car and approached the front door.

"We got a call about a disturbance," said the first officer.

"Officers, we need an ambulance right away. My friend attacked us and ruined part of his home. My friend over here shot him. He's not responding."

The second officer turned away to call an ambulance to the scene.

The first officer gripped his gun, eyeing Mitch. "Sir, please step forward. Do you have the firearm with you?"

Mitch eyed Cliff, who'd taken his gun. Cliff handed it to the officer.

"Thank you. Now I need to—" The officer stopped and drew his weapon. "Hold it right there, sir."

Dennis stood at the top of the porch stairs, arms raised, damp from the blood covering his chest. The blue mass had grown significantly since his friends had last seen him lying in the entrance to the living room. It now clung to his neck and around his upper chest. He stepped slowly toward his friends.

"You gotta be fucking kidding," Mitch said.

Omar and Cliff stepped away, getting closer to the officer who had Dennis in his crosshairs.

"I am one but will become whole. I am one but will become whole. I am one but will become whole." Dennis repeated this with each step he took, bringing him closer to the officers.

The second officer drew his weapon, coming to the aid of his partner.

"Sir, stop, or I'll use force." The officers cocked their guns.

Dennis didn't slow down.

"Freeze or we will shoot!"

The second officer fired, ripping into Dennis' chest.

The blue mass extended out of Dennis' fingertips and launched the officer into the side of his squad car. The windows exploded, and glass flew all across the yard.

The first officer fired several shots and his back exploded as Dennis punctured his chest with the blue mass. Dennis' other arm reached out, opening a second hole in the officer's chest above the first, splitting the man in half. Blood pooled onto the yard before seeping into the soil, leaving the decapitated body to soak in its own fluids.

Mitch didn't waste a second; he picked his gun up off the ground and aimed it at Dennis. "This isn't Dennis anymore, and I'm not waiting around to die!" The bullets exploded from the barrel, flying into Dennis' arms, legs, chest, and neck.

"Mitch, get away from him!" Cliff said, stopping Omar before he could get any closer.

Omar met Cliff's terrified glare.

"Let's get out of here while we still have a chance. Leave Mitch if he wants to be the hero," Cliff said.

"Why would we leave without him?" Omar asked.

"He's going to get us killed. We need to get help."

Omar got closer to Cliff, stunned by his response. "Help? Dennis just killed two cops. What other help can we get?"

"That's my point. He didn't kill us. We must mean more to him than those police did. There has to be something we're missing," Cliff said.

Mitch's body slammed into the porch, cracking the post supporting the awning. Cliff and Omar stared in horror as the roof of the porch caved in, burying both Mitch and Dennis in the rubble.

"Come on and help me with this!" Omar ran to the porch and started pulling pieces of the roof off the steps. He moved large chunks and tossed them aside.

Cliff admired his determination to help even the biggest asshole of their group. Omar's heart was as big as his physique. Cliff was only good at running, so his efforts at removing pieces of roofing were hardly effective.

Cliff threw several pieces away and uncovered Mitch's arm. He pointed and alerted Omar. "Here, help me pull him up."

Omar pulled with all his strength, flexing his bulging arms even further. Cliff felt useless with his colossal friend doing all the work.

Mitch stood up from the rubble and handed his gun to Cliff. Omar helped Mitch clear his feet from the porch and stand on top of the wreckage.

"I'm good. Let go," Mitch said.

Omar stepped back and let Mitch catch his breath.

They all took in the sight of the destroyed front porch, knowing their friend buried beneath was probably dead. Then the pile creaked, alarming the friends of an impending collapse.

"Mitch, come on. This whole thing is about to give out," Omar said, extending his hand.

"Yeah, I'm coming." Mitch stepped forward and then froze, looking like he was holding his breath.

Cliff stepped toward his stubborn friend. "What are you waiting for? Let's go—"

A blue mass, semi-resembling a human hand, exploded out of the rubble and covered Mitch's head. He threw his head back, screaming a muffled cry from beneath the blue aggressor. The arm lifted Mitch from his feet, holding him in the air. Dennis, or what remained of their friend, emerged from the wreckage, revealing a maniacal smile.

"Now, I have become two." Dennis swung his blue mutated leg into Omar and Cliff, throwing them to the ground.

The blue mass covering his arm pulsated, steady as an athlete's heartbeat. Mitch's skin sagged as if he were aging rapidly. His flesh drooped as it withered. But his torso remained intact, his body sliding toward the blue entity. A thumping sound pounded from the creature's chest, vibrating the shingles and wooden slabs beneath its feet.

Cliff and Omar got up and fled, withdrawing steadily from the scene.

"Omar, it wants to absorb us. That thing didn't kill Dennis. It's using him as a host to become stronger," Cliff said.

"Why us? Why kill the cops and leave us?"

"It recognizes our bond, our strengths, our weaknesses," Cliff said. "Dennis was the brain, so it must've started there. Mitch was the ego, the one who faced anything with his chest out in front."

Omar glanced at Cliff and down at himself. "Now he needs brawn and speed."

Cliff nodded. "I don't really know how we can stop or get away from it."

"You can't." The entity approached them rapidly. "I am two, but I will become whole. You are the last two pieces that will make me complete. Do not fight it. Do not resist what is fate!"

"That sounds like Mitch in there," Omar said. "What do we do?"

"We run. It doesn't have our speed. We go as far as we can and hide out until we figure out what to do."

Cliff took off. Omar broke into a sprint and tried to keep up with Cliff. They ran together for several minutes before finding shelter behind the abandoned house at the edge of their street. Omar was winded, desperately trying to catch his breath, while Cliff's breathing remained steady. Cliff rested his hand on Omar's back while he was bent over, gasping for air.

"Hey, try and be quiet. That thing will hear us."

"I'm trying, but I'm not as—"

Blue fingers curled around Omar's neck, lifting him off the ground. Cliff rushed the entity, trying to force it to loosen its grip, but didn't stand a chance. Omar gripped the limb, working to pry his way free. His efforts only made his energy drain faster. He barreled his fist into it, swinging with all his strength.

The glowing fingers closed tighter, and Omar's grip began to loosen.

Cliff watched in horror, slowly stepping back as the creature—which now didn't resemble Dennis at all—gripped and pulled Omar closer.

The blue mass slowly covered Omar's arms.

"I need your brute strength to become whole."

"Kill me, you fucking slimy shitbag! I'm not letting you take me!" Omar yelled.

With a smile, the creature opened its mouth, launching its razor-sharp tongue into Omar's mouth.

"Your death won't aid in my completion. Your pain, however, is a treat I'll take proudly."

The tongue pierced through the back of his head, pinning Omar to the house. Omar's arms went limp before they disappeared into electric-blue sleeves.

Cliff took off running, not waiting for the same fate as his friends.

"One. Final. Piece."

The baritone voice of the creature was close behind Cliff, haunting him to his core. His legs helped him steadily stretch the distance between him and whatever it was that had consumed his former friends. He didn't want to stop and think about his neighbors, who turned out to be great friends, and wouldn't be there when he woke up in the morning.

A clearing in the yard ahead invited Cliff to stop and rest. The house was quiet, and little to no sound followed his push through the weeds at the edge of the property line.

He grasped his knees, steadying his breathing.

Panic radiated into his core. His three friends were dead, and he had to fend for himself. The wives wouldn't be back for several more hours, so they'd be of no help with surviving the night. He had nowhere to go. Inside that being were three people who knew him better than anyone else.

A faint rustle alarmed Cliff. Birds emerged from the trees and soared like a black wave into the night sky. The air was silent.

Suddenly, something collided with Cliff's chest, sending him flying into a tree. He heard a loud snap and slid down the tree as air fled his lungs. Ribs punctured his shirt, blood flowing down to legs. He was too weak to continue.

The creature emerged from the trees. It had grown, more resembling Omar. The blue color pulsed, the dimming light feeding off the remaining parts of Cliff's friend. It stood over Cliff, who couldn't have resisted if he'd tried.

The baritone rumble of its voice vibrated Cliff's body. "All is one." The blue entity stood on Cliff's legs. He was grateful he couldn't feel it, but he still feared his final moments.

"Please. Kill. Me." Cliff mustered up the three words as blood filled his mouth.

The creature stepped forward to take in the last flesh puzzle piece, and the sky's vibrant electric color returned. Several bursts of blue made the sky glow like daylight. It took the creature's attention, shrieking into the air. The sound was too hard for Cliff to handle. Tears filled his eyes, and he succumbed to the inevitable death that was upon him.

The shrieking continued to amplify.

Bats fled their dark corners, and car alarms erupted.

Blue bursts of lightning crashed in the sky. They dropped into the suburban streets like crashing planes. Homes burst into flames and telephone poles fell to the ground, illuminating the neighborhood. The invasion was on its way.

Cliff wiped his wet eyes in time to see the appendage latch on and swallow both of his legs.

The blue mass coated the final bits of his body and then they stood tall on powerful legs. They glowed like lightning, becoming a beacon in the night. And then they looked to the sky, shrieking into the air.

"I am whole. Now the remaining can join me."

As Cliff's eyes were swallowed, his final view was the electric blue consuming the night air that he and his friends enjoyed one final time.

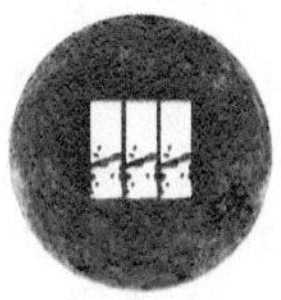

BATTLE OF EARTH'S END

The shriek echoed into the silence of night. The noise, unlike anything Tyler had heard in the neighborhood prior to that night, rattled him. He lowered the volume on his speakers, making sure it wasn't the background noise of his game playing tricks on his exhausted ears. After several seconds, he returned to the game in which he'd invested many hours.

A loud crash followed the sound, and Tyler jumped up from his seat. Even with his bulky gaming headphones on, he'd heard it well. It had been close.

"Fuck, did you guys hear that?" he said, through his microphone.

"Yeah, did your drunk mom face plant into the coffee table again?" Billy shrieked laughter.

Tyler lowered the volume more. Billy was known for annunciating his jokes more than he needed to, but people still responded to them well.

Laughter broke out among their chat.

"Eat shit, Billy. My mom's asleep," Tyler said.

He hated confiding in unreliable friends, but they often invited him to games because they needed people, not because they actually liked Tyler. He liked having the gaming company, but it wasn't always pleasantries. Tyler would never admit it, but falling asleep crying because the "white trash" kid ruined their game comments really dug deep. He was good at dishing it back, so that helped cover his emotions, but that didn't make it any easier to bear.

"Probably by the toilet, trailer boy," Billy shot back at Tyler.

"Hey, Billy. The only reason you're in this game is because you have the best setup for hangout," Jamie said. "Leave Tyler alone or I'll wreck you again in one on one. Get it together and try to last longer in royale."

Jamie was the toughest girl they'd ever known. She'd hung out with her brothers and picked up on their gaming, quickly beating them and most of the guys at school. Only one or two came close to her, but they often invited her into competitions or frequent all weekend sessions.

"Fuck you, bitch. You're lucky you're a girl who can play good," Billy shot back.

"Gotta carry your shitty playing. Tyler, you down for another round?"

"Hold on. Let me go check on that noise." Tyler dropped the volume to a lower level before another insult from Billy could dig deeper into him. He stood, waiting to hear anything else. By this time, close to midnight, his mom was lying curled up on the couch after her fourth or fifth glass of wine.

"Mom, are you up?"

Tyler crept into the living room, not wanting to find his mom had fallen through the coffee table again. He didn't want to relive another weekend at the hospital, wondering if she would bleed to death while he waited for her.

Luckily, she was fast asleep, snoring, with her empty glass on the floor with a splash of red wine staining the carpet. He'd do his best to clean it up for her by the time she woke in the morning.

Tyler grabbed the glass and placed it in the sink. He noticed the blue lights falling from the sky all over the neighborhood, and the faint bit of smoke coming from his neighbor's upstairs window.

Tyler rushed to wake his mom. "Mom, Mom, the neighbor's house is on fire. Didn't they ask you to watch it while they're away?" She didn't budge at all. "Mom, get up!"

As hard as he tried, Tyler's mom was deep in her alcohol induced rest, and would be until her fierce hangover pulled her up the next morning.

Tyler pulled his phone from his pocket and dialed his dad. It rang for longer than he'd like.

"Pick up the phone!"

He didn't expect to hear anything other than the voicemail message. Tyler's dad had left months ago and didn't answer much. It drove his mom to drink, being the sole provider after nearly fifteen years of marriage. She hardly spoke of the grieving she did in her own time, leaving Tyler to deal with his overwhelming emotions on his own.

The voicemail message started.

"Fuck!" Tyler slammed his cell phone down, shattering the screen. "Shit. Shit."

The phone had little hope for recovery with the spiderwebbed cracks covering most of the screen. Try as he might, he got little response when he tried to dial his dad again. No hope of getting anything out of it, he sat it aside.

"Fuck you too, Dad," Tyler said.

He glanced over at his mom, feeling the sadness overwhelm him, thinking of how little his dad wanted to be there for either of them. He sat at the edge of the couch, watching as she breathed in her inebriated slumber. She had more stress on her shoulders than she could handle, trying to manage the house with her collapsed marriage on her mind.

Another crash rattled the house. Several more came shortly after.

"The game," he said, suddenly remembering.

Tyler rushed to his room, raising the volume, and heard his friends' banter once again.

"Guys, are you still there?"

"Fuck, Tyler. Where were you? Are you seeing this shit outside? My mom is practically shitting her pants over this!" Billy shrieked loud enough for Tyler to drop the volume again.

"Seriously, dude. I think it's you shitting," Jamie retorted. "Tyler, tell me you're watching this."

Tyler peered out his window and saw the hovering blue masses light up the sky. He wasn't quite sure what they were, but to him they resembled mounds of jelly or fun putty he used to play with when he was much younger. The electric blue was brighter than fireworks any of them had seen. The masses collapsed on cars, left holes in the sidewalks, ripped through power lines. Several bold neighbors stepped out of their front doors and looked up to behold the vibrant colored descension.

"Ain't catching me outside for this shit. Who knows what could happen if that shit touches you. Growing fingers from your arms and face."

"I think one of those things got into my neighbor's house. Jamie, can you get over here? Can't go in there on my own," Tyler said.

"Scared, pussy?" Billy laughed.

"Don't want to get trapped by myself if something goes wrong, asshole," Tyler said. He'd been on his last nerve rethinking his attempt to speak with his father.

"I'll be there in ten minutes," Jamie said. "My dad won't be out of work for another two hours or so. Signing off."

Jamie's mic went quiet, and she exited the game. Tyler didn't feel the need to say goodbye to Billy, so he followed the same way.

Tyler rushed outside and watched the hovering glow in the sky from his porch. He squinted as the blue blobs glowed brighter as it fell. In the distance, he thought he heard an ominous shriek. It wasn't a sound he was familiar with—a screeching tire, a frightened cat, or a child screaming. This was something very different.

A rapid flow of blue descension followed the shriek. The blue piles scattered the street in all directions, sitting idle with no sign of reaction to the noise. A faint glow spread across the sky—a different color than the blinding blue. It was purple, glowing in a massive sphere, and it felt like it was meant for Tyler's eyes only.

It flashed, and then it was gone.

"Tyler! Hey!"

His fixation of the purple stopped when he heard Jamie pedaling quickly toward his house.

"Okay, what do we got?" she asked.

Tyler pointed to his neighbor's house. "My neighbor, Omar. His window, second floor. It might be one of those blue things."

"Well, let's get going!" Jamie dropped her bike and walked in front of Tyler. He always admired her bravery. It was a trait he'd never acquired.

They opened the front door and the smell of burnt wood wafted past their noses immediately. The floor creaked beneath their feet as they walked up the stairs. The top step gave them all the answers they needed.

A vibrant glow fed light into the hallway. It pulsed, in and out, slowly building in tempo.

"What the hell is it?" Tyler said. "Space slime? Kind of looks like that movie The Blob."

"Could be. I think when it crashed into the house that caused the fire. Must've fizzled out on its own."

Jamie reached out to touch the blue.

"Hey, don't do that! You don't know what it is!"

"Dude, you're as timid as Billy thinks you are. Calm down." Jamie stepped back from the slime.

"Shut up! No, I'm not. Just don't want you getting eaten by something like that."

The shriek came again. This time, it sounded louder.

Closer.

"What…? What the hell was that?" Jamie asked.

"I'm not sure, but I heard it twice before you got to my house."

They looked out the nearby window, walking away from the space slime. A creature resembling a massive beast stood in the grass across from Omar's house. It stood taller than a grizzly bear, with towering arms that could fight like a gorilla.

It shrieked into the air again, louder, with a different pitch this time.

The shriek went on for so long, Jamie and Tyler suspected it would bring more people outside.

And it did.

The Tompkins stood on their porch and watched.

Several people turned on their lights or gazed out their windows. The Tompkins took a chance, and exited their home then watched the invasion transpire from their front porch.

As the shrieking continued, the glowing masses rose into the air, levitating higher above the houses. Jamie and Tyler looked on as the one beside them rose from the floor through the partially destroyed roof.

Jamie gripped Tyler's hand. She wasn't known for being romantic in the slightest. At best, she had tougher skin than most of the boys her age. Tyler ignored the possible invasion going on and fell into the moment, holding her hand.

He had never felt this way about a girl before. Maybe it was their friendship evolving, or maybe it was the part of Jamie she hadn't shown to Tyler before. He didn't know; he didn't care. He just wanted this.

Glancing back across the street, he noticed they were doing the exact same thing as their neighbors were—watching without any idea what would happen next.

The blue giant stopped its shriek, and the masses shot toward the nearby homes.

Glass exploded from windows, and the screams filled the night air. People ran from their homes and frantically ran about outside.

"Tyler, watch out!" Jamie shoved Tyler down to the ground and then dove out of the way.

A mass split in two before plummeting to the top floor where they peered out, sliding up their legs up to their knees, gripping firmly.

"Fuck! Fuck! What's happening?" Tyler shouted.

Jamie held her hand up, insinuating for Tyler to stop moving. "Don't do anything. See what happens."

The slime tried to bind together again but didn't connect. They released Tyler and Jamie, and crawled down to the street. They watched it escape.

"What do you think that was?" Tyler asked.

"It didn't want to connect us. Maybe we aren't a match or something?"

The neighbors fled. The Konnors ran out together, soaked in blue, trying to get away from one another as the binding started to connect them, pulling them close to assimilate each piece of the family.

"Look! It keeps people close by likeness," Tyler said.

The Konnors—Mickey and Sadie, along with their son, Martin—tried moving in three different directions as the blue pulled them into the growing mass.

It pulled aggressively, launching the three back and pulling them into one giant puddle. As the substance swallowed them, it formed into a figure like the shrieking blue giant. It stood tall, shorter than the largest but taller than six feet. It let out a higher-pitched shriek, standing behind its leader.

"Holy shit! It eats families and turns them into that!" Jamie said.

"Can you get ahold of your dad?" Tyler asked.

"Doubt it. I have a plan. Let's get over to Billy's. Worst case scenario, we can hide in that rich fuck's house."

Tyler immediately thought about his mom. He had to look out for her because no one else would. His eyes watered, thinking of her alone on the couch.

She pulled his arm. "Tyler, your mom will be fine just being shit-faced, laying on the couch. Let's go."

Tyler snapped his arm back. "She's not shit-faced. Fuck you."

It took everything in him to hold back from sobbing. He hoped Jamie didn't tell the assholes at school he cried so often. He didn't find any value in bottling up his emotions like most boys his age were often told to.

"Hey, I'm sorry," she said. "But she'll be fine. She's safer by herself. Billy's place is our best bet. Let's go."

She flew down the stairs without waiting for Tyler's response.

Tyler wasn't a leader, so he followed behind her.

They got on their bikes and pedaled down the street, avoiding several creatures made from consumed neighborhood families.

"Don't you think it's weird we haven't heard any sirens?" Tyler asked.

"Middle of the night? Probably only a few officers on duty. Blues probably got most of them stuck at their homes."

Blues?

"That's a good name," Tyler said. "I was thinking about globs myself."

Billy's home was at the end of a winding driveway. He often bragged his dad made a lot of money, trying to further insult Tyler any chance he got. The large home appeared quiet, all lights welcoming anyone who approached. Several blues were scattered across the yard.

Jamie screeched to a halt beside Billy's family's luxury Range Rover. "Let me call this dipshit."

Billy's phone rang twice before answering. "Yo, is Tyler still alive? This shit is crazy."

"We're both outside your house," Jamie said. "Come let us in."

Billy's window overlooked the driveway. He looked out, greeted by Jamie's middle finger. Tyler couldn't help but laugh at the gesture. She was as crazy as Tyler thought, but he loved every second of being around her.

"Fuck no," Billy said. "Dad doesn't want those things getting in. Besides, you both have homes to hide in."

Blues rose into the air. They hovered closer to the front of the house.

"Billy, who else is home with you?" Jamie asked.

"My parents and my brother. Why?"

Glass exploded from the windows as invaders flew inside. Jamie heard screams echo from the phone.

Gunshots followed. Globs of blue splattered the front bay window.

Billy's dad ran outside. "Suzie, let's go!"

"We need to get the boys," she screamed from the front door, running to the driveway. She wore a guilty expression for abandoning her boys, which her selfish husband seemed unable to share.

"Fred can take Billy," the dad yelled. He turned to the upstairs window, firing two shots. "Boys! We need to go!"

Tyler watched in disgust, ashamed their father could be so cruel to his kids.

Then he noticed the purple glow from earlier that night in his peripheral vision. It pulsated as he turned to gaze at it. It had grown into a small ball that now fell upon the house. The roof split, and the front of the house crashed to the lawn where it shattered into large fragments that soared past Jamie and Tyler. Billy's mother's screams were quickly silenced when the house erupted in purple light, followed by fire.

The house quickly melted beneath the blaze. Neither Billy nor Fred left the house, and their parents' car slowly drove off down the driveway.

Blue globs pulled themselves out of the house, screeching from the fires burning their flesh.

The purple thing pulsed again, sending bursts

of energy against its blue foe, melting flesh until their movement stopped entirely. The purple being, glowing in a bright light, stepped out from the now fiery lot that was once a luxurious home.

Billy's parents drove away, but Tyler noticed blue scattered across the trunk. The purple figure flew past Jamie and him, exploding the car into a fireball. Billy's parents were consumed immediately.

"Holy shit! Holy shit!" Tyler panicked, backing up against a truck that had survived the attack.

The creature turned, taking in both Jamie and Tyler.

Tyler screamed, but Jamie quickly covered his mouth.

She pushed him back against the truck.

"Fucking relax! Don't let it see your fear."

Jamie turned back to the figure standing before her. She showed no fear.

'Are you two all alone?' the thing said.

"Holy shit! Did you just talk inside my head?" Tyler stepped back, looking at the figure with intrigue. Communicating telepathically wasn't in his knowledge of aliens or beings from other worlds, and he was curious to further expand on what he knew of aliens.

"I heard it, too. This is wild." Jamie looked up at the creature, smiling wide. "So, do I speak out loud to you or do I just think about what I have to say?" Jamie asked.

The being looked at her confused.

'Either way, I will understand. You humans fascinate me.'

"Where did you come from?"

'Great distances away from here. I was nearly blown back from your shuttle explosion above Earth.'

"Shuttle? What shuttle?" Jamie asked. She turned to Tyler. "Any idea what it's talking about? You're a space nerd."

Tyler stepped in front of Jamie. "Are you talking about the Sempiternal? I heard on the news they lost communication with them months ago."

'It's true. Despite their extreme efforts, the humans weren't successful with destroying me.'

"What are these things? Where did they come from?"

'An old foe. We fought once before, but it seems they've deemed humanity vulnerable and for their taking. I won't let that happen.'

Jamie and Tyler were overwhelmed with questions, but the being flew off into the night, fighting off its adversaries and leaving the two kids to fend for themselves.

"Great. What do we do now?" Tyler asked.

Jamie picked up her bike, mounting it. "Come on, we need an expert."

Tyler pedaled his bike to Jamie.

"I think it's time we paid some respect to the town conspiracy theorist," she said.

Tyler was onboard with talking to Terrence, the one who constantly shouted about aliens, the government, and chemicals in the water. Everyone told the kids to stay away from him, but the time had come to listen to him.

Jamie and Tyler got to the end of Katrine Trailer Park despite plenty of distractions. The fire department was overwhelmed with house fires started by the blues. The few police who made appearances had either been decapitated by creatures or lay sprawled out in the street in numerous parts. Several who were still living dealt with the invaders by shooting them with their pistols and the occasional shotgun, neither of which did much damage, if at all.

The neighborhood was filled with the screams from fleeing, or dying, families and screeching tires.

The monstrosities had absorbed many people, continuing to tear through houses for remaining family members.

"Tyler, we're almost there!" Jamie swung her arm in the air.

She pointed to the last row of trailers. That was where Terrence had his modified security cameras, antennas, and a makeshift security door he had welded to the front of his trailer.

Terrence stood outside, burning the piles off his front steps with a flamethrower.

"Not a chance in hell of taking me, you blue cesspools!" he said. "The great purple being will be your destroyer!"

Terrence scanned the area, torching every last blue invader he came across. Apparently satisfied that he'd gotten all he could, he dropped the flamethrower and let out a loud sigh as the weight was relieved from his thin frame.

"Terrence!" Jamie shouted, dropping her bike in front of the torched blues.

She hopped over a few melted blues, barely evading the flames licking at her jeans. Tyler's stop was more abrupt, falling inches away from a burning heap, feeling the heat singe his eyebrows.

"Jamie? Why aren't you home? The invasion has begun. By my calculations, these things will take over the entire town by morning unless they're stopped. These beasts seem less interested in people like me, who've made the wise decision to live alone and more interested in families, as I imagined they would. I always said attachments are liabilities!"

Tyler was curious about how much time Jamie had spent with Terrence, seeing as she already knew him on a first name basis. That and the fact he was divulging unusual information to her about the invasion he claimed to have known about prior to tonight.

"Do you guys know each other?" Tyler asked.

Jamie pointed at Terrence's trailer. "I come to the space station at least once a month. He gives me all the good alien movie recommendations."

Terrence rolled his eyes. "Stop calling it a space station, Jamie! I told you it's the Info Hub!" He picked up the flamethrower again. "Now, if you'll excuse me… I'm taking this trailer park back as its rightful owner and leader! People are going to respect me once they see I was right all along!"

"Wait… Right about what?" Tyler asked.

Terrence and Jamie stared at one another before Jamie gave Terrence a nod. They both looked back at Tyler.

"Terrence, he's cool," she said. "Let's show him."

Terrence nodded. "Right this way. Don't touch anything inside. My experiments could all be lost with reckless human contact." He waved them to the front door.

Terrence moved a white board on wheels out from behind his computer. It was split in two sections with one side solely devoted to the purple invader they'd seen earlier, and the other side was for the blue masses. Several blurry photos of both invaders were scattered across the board.

His retractable pointer slapped on the hard surface filled from top to bottom with pictures.

"Now, these blue globs, piles, mounds…whatever you want to call them…They're known as the Molders. They feed on other life forms and use their energy to evolve. Finding like-minded groups, people with DNA matches, similar tribes, stuff like that. It helps them grow bigger, stronger. Families. Liabilities, like I said."

Terrence swung his pointer around without giving them a chance to speak, starting on the purple image. "This guy…we only know as a single being. Never spotted another of his species. Not yet, anyway. It can replicate some of its abilities if it chooses or give other beings its powers. Some claim it was born from Nebula dust, a mixture of dead stars that formed and created this unbeatable specimen."

"The *Sempiternal*. Do you think he was involved in whatever went down there?" Tyler asked.

Terrence got in Tyler's face. "Everything is connected. Don't you understand? One lifeform finds Earth for its harvest, and the other tries to get a feel for humanity by taking down the shuttle on its way to the surface. Now, they somehow coincidentally arrive on the same night in the early hours before dusk? Grow up, kid. This invasion is well past the beginning stages!"

Tyler glanced over at Jamie. *He really spends too much time diving into these alien theories*, he thought.

"So what does that mean? Are we team blue or team purple?" Jamie asked.

Terrence pulled the blinds out slightly, glancing out at the trailer park. The night sky still glowed blue, like when they'd first arrived. Distant screams could be heard between the mobile homes.

"Only one purple guy," Terrence said. "My money says he won't feast on me. However, I don't trust anyone except you two." Terrence retracted his pointer as he looked back at them.

Bang!

An explosion erupted in the trailer park, sending Tyler and Jamie to the floor.

Terrence slid the blinds aside again, showing several trailers at the end of the lot had been crushed. A blue giant, maybe the same one from Tyler's street, rose to its feet, screaming into the sky. Several more beasts came to its aid. The sky lit up with a vibrant purple luminescence as the creature descended on its foe.

Jamie and Terrence both watched on.

"I bet that's the blue giant Tyler and I saw earlier," Jamie said. "Will Aluben be able to beat all of these Molders?"

"Aluben?" Tyler asked.

"I figure it's better to name it instead of calling it the 'purple guy'."

"Why 'Aluben'? What does that mean?"

Before Jamie could answer Tyler, Terrence chided in. "Nebula backwards. Brilliant."

The screaming intensified as the beasts shrieked at the glowing purple consuming the sky.

Another blast shook the trailer park. The beasts were buried into the ground as Aluben forced them down. Nearby mobile homes exploded, and debris from the fight bombarded Terrence's trailer.

Terrence covered Jamie, and Tyler dropped to the ground.

Tears stung Tyler's eyes.

Terrence grabbed a bag from under his couch, checking the pockets. "I'm out of here in five minutes or I'm going to be stranded. Or worse…dead."

Terrence snapped, pointing at the door. "I wish I could save you both. Whatever time we have left on this planet, the strong must survive. I have to get to my bunker. You may follow me if you'd like, but I'm no hero."

The ground shook again. Blinding purple illuminated the windows.

A loud hum followed. "On the floor…Now!"

Terrence tipped over his coffee table. Tyler's tears flowed heavily now as he hid beside Jamie, beneath the rolled over couch. Terrence pulled them both close. "Looks like I'm stuck with you two for the end of the world."

The table's legs slid under the couch, forming a cage to keep them safe. Forced into one another, the three were shielded from the fiery blast. The roof ripped from the trailer. Then the walls rattled as they folded inward, burying the three below the rubble.

●

Tyler opened his eyes and saw Jamie's hand reaching for him. Jamie pulled him out from under the tattered couch, grunting as she struggled to hold her grip.

Shrieking and faint whimpers were all he could hear over the crackling flames.

"Come on, Tyler. Give me some help!" Jamie pulled her weakened friend from the rubble until Terrence could push himself from under the furniture.

Tyler wiped his eyes. "Jamie, I have to go see if my mom is okay. I have to check on her."

"Tyler—"

"Please, I need to make sure she isn't hurt. Or worse—"

"Tyler. Open your eyes," Jamie said.

Tyler hadn't realized he was only staring at Jamie and seeing the flames in his peripheral vision. He looked around the now decimated trailer park, noticing the flames had consumed what remained of the flattened homes. The Molders rose from wreckage. Aluben stood in front of the alpha—the blue giant who towered high, illuminating through the fires and darkness—longtime enemies facing one another on a new planet. And Tyler's small town—their new battlefield—was on the brink of collapse.

The giant let out its piercing shriek, making Tyler and Jamie cover their ears.

"Hey, where is Terrence?" Tyler asked.

Then they saw him outside. Terrence pulled a large crate from the trunk of his crushed car, crouched low while opening the locks and latches. The lid swung open, and he pulled out the fuel canister.

This flamethrower was heavier than the last. It made sense Terrence would have another.

Aluben rose above the blue giant, and the smaller, fully formed Molders lined up behind their master. The purple entity illuminated and then descended upon its enemy, sending the giant deep into the ground. The Molders swarmed Aluben, their bodies boiling as a purple blast scorched their blue flesh. They fell one by one, toppling over their leader.

Terrence whistled to Jamie and Tyler. They ran to him, ducking beneath the back of the car next to him.

"Even if Aluben has the strength, they're going to outnumber him. There's no telling how many more of these things are out there!"

"Can we help at all?" Jamie asked.

"I'm sure as hell going to try!" Terrence gestured to his flamethrower. He slid the canister into the base, lighting the flame at the end, and gave a quick blast to check that it worked.

Tyler flinched.

"You two, gather up any liquor bottles you can find lying around and any clothing you see," Terrence said. "Stuff a piece of cloth in the bottle, light it on fire, and throw it. Get a few of those in your artillery and we can give this guy a fighting chance. Go!"

Terrence crept closer to the battlefield, staying out of sight.

"Tyler, I know being brave isn't normally your thing, but we're about to help save the goddamn world. Think you can hold it together?"

Tyler hated how scared he was as much as anyone else. He no longer expected to see his parents again, so the only people he had now were Terrence and Jamie. Even with the fight persisting and the Molders splattering all around him, he wanted to help. He would do anything he could to save Jamie and save the world with Terrence.

"Just tell me what to do, and we can kill these assholes!" he said.

"Grab as many liquor bottles as you can find," Jamie said, "and I'll start grabbing scattered clothing. Meet back here in five minutes."

"Got it!" Tyler ran to the burning trailers, scavenging anything that might be of use while the fight continued in the field only feet away. He glanced at Terrence to see how he was doing.

Terrence crept closer to the line of battle, staying clear of any Molders readying for another round of combat. He paced himself, squatting down low while holding the flamethrower close to his chest.

As the battle pushed on, the park adjacent to the trailers had become a warzone. Uprooted trees were now slimed with blue drippings. The grass, a popular spot for picnics, was now riddled with mounds of dirt and a crater nearly fifty feet wide. The blue Molders continued to add width to the opening. And Aluben wasn't slowing down against its old nemesis. Streaks of blue slime coated everything, yet there was seldom a purple splatter anywhere.

'Not even with all of your strength could you defeat me.'
The blue giant stepped from the large crater, roaring into the sky, louder than it had before. It raised its arms, drawing in more energy as it flexed.

That thing has some serious muscle. It reminds me of my neighbor, Omar, Tyler thought.

The Molders crawled toward their leader, slowly linking their masses. They merged into their master, building onto the bulk. The resulting being towered over Aluben, nearly thirty feet high. It gripped Aluben's throat, lifting him into the air. Inches away from the monster's face, Aluben charged his power, illuminating once again.

Aluben's illuminating dimmed as this new being squeezed. Then it thrust Aluben down into the dirt, held there by the behemoth creature. As it released its grip, its fist descended into Aluben's head, forcing him deeper into the dirt mound.

Terrence glanced at Jamie. "Now or never, kiddos. Aluben needs some support!"

Jamie and Tyler proceeded to shove several pieces of cloth into whatever liquor bottles they'd found. Jamie lit them from one of the small fires burning in the flattened trailer park.

"Ready?" Jamie handed Tyler a bottle.

"Absolutely." Tyler hurled the first Molotov cocktail at the beast, where it shattered and erupted fireballs onto its slimy blue skin. The thunderous roar pulled its attention from Aluben, turning its fiery shriek on its human adversaries.

The remaining beasts ran past their leader and charged the decimated mobile homes.

"Keep tossing more bottles!" Terrence pointed to the edge of the lot where the grass started.

Tyler and Jamie did as told, their handmade bombs creating a fiery barricade between Terrence and the beasts. Their shrieking intensified, and the kids covered their ears. Even that didn't help much.

"This should help that sore throat!" Terrence swung the barrel of his flamethrower around and shot flames out at the charging Molders. The blazing wall towered over them, but the intensity of the creatures' screams and whimpers gave Tyler confidence. He knew they were winning the battle.

Several Molders dropped and pounded the ground as the fire blasted them, melting them. Some in the back retreated, only their limbs singed as they headed back to the alpha.

It wasn't long until the blue giant turned its attention on Terrence and charged forward.

Terrence fired up his flamethrower again and ignited the approaching creature. It slowed, trying to shield itself from the heavy flow of fire. Terrence moved forward, holding the trigger firmly and fully blasting heat at the colossal monstrosity.

Terrence ignored the screams. This was Terrence's moment to fight the invader with his fiery rage.

Over the years, Tyler had heard all the whispers about the weirdo, conspiracy theorist, obsessive

Terrence. Kids laughed at him and threw eggs at his trailer, but Tyler never bought into any of that, and now he saw another side of Terrence. Besides, most of the people who'd had something to say about the neighborhood oddball were probably dead or sucked into a Molder by now.

And there were bigger concerns. How much of the planet was on the brink of collapse? Was it just this small town that had seen the initial invasion? Was first contact with these creatures made here, or were the Molders slowly picking off places around the globe? Either way, Tyler was on the forefront of the battle, and he prayed he was on the winning team.

"You don't scare me, space demon," Terrence said. "I am here to bring the fires of humanity down upon you! I am your destroyer! I shall—"

A crushing blow struck Terrence's chest and sent him flying into the air.

The flamethrower fell from his grip and seemed to drop for an eternity. Terrence descended rapidly, plummeting to the ground like a crashing meteor.

The blue giant returned its attention to Aluben's location. The Molders returned to their leader, evading the scorching wall that blocked Tyler and Jamie. But they were both focused on where Terrence landed because he remained still. He was just lying there staring into the empty sky, no indication that he was alive or just immobilized. Then he moved, just a little twist of his neck as he took in his damaged body.

"Tyler, come on. He needs our help!" Jamie walked around the flames, rushing to Terrence's aid.

As Tyler and Jamie grew closer, they heard Terrence groaning, but he wasn't drawing any of the Molders' attention. The battle between blue and purple waged on as Jamie crouched down, checking on Terrence.

Jamie propped up his head. "Hey, Terrence. You alive in there?"

Terrence nodded weakly.

"Aluben better win, though, or I'm toast."

Blinding purple light flooded the field. The blue giant went airborne and descended upon Aluben, knocking it deeper into the ground.

Molders scattered into the trees as the ground shook, throwing Jamie and Tyler off their feet. The rumbling pushed the Molders back further. Then the ground split open, the pavement cracking. The openings glowed a bright purple, and Aluben rose from beneath. The hole was now deeper than before.

The blue giant crashed into the ground beside Aluben and roared at his purple adversary. The blast threw it into the sky again and Aluben rose high to watch the giant crash down into the treetops. The remaining beasts scurried into the trees, vanishing.

Aluben floated to Terrence's battered body.

Tyler heard the voice in his head again. He knew Jamie and Terrence could hear it too, giving their attention as it spoke.

'Your weak attempt at battling a superior being is admirable. I have newfound respect for you humans.'

"That's great and all," Jamie said, "but that thing is going to overpower you or worse, outnumber you. You can't stop them all."

'Then I shall increase my numbers. I believe you all can carry the fight with me.'

Aluben's charge radiated, letting out bursts of bright light. He gripped Tyler and Terrence's leg. Tyler couldn't believe the feeling of power coursing through his body going stiff with the surging energy. Jamie, still holding Terrence, shot upright as did Tyler and Terrence. Tyler looked at his fingers and saw tiny bolts dancing about his digits.

Terrence appeared to have returned to his normal self, the bones audibly snapping back into place and the torn flesh healing.

'My powers, my healing. You are my equals, my soldiers.'

Terrence stood, admiring the new energy and dancing bolts on his hands. Jamie watched the lightning dance around her fingertips, shooting small bolts into the ground. Tyler, feeling the weightlessness, pushed off the ground, and floated freely.

"Do you realize what this means, guys?" Jamie asked.

"We're motherfucking badass alien superheroes. That's what!" Tyler yelled.

"We're gods. Like him. Like Aluben. Let's take this world back."

Bright blue streaks of lightning filled the sky, striking everywhere at once. The glow moved closer to the center of town. Smoke filled the sky as homes, cars, and businesses all were lost to the fiery attack.

Aluben rose higher than his newfound fighters. Terrence kicked off the ground, floating to the height of Aluben. Jamie and Tyler followed.

'They're leveling the remaining parts of your town. They know they can't win unless they destroy it all.'

The blue giant could be seen in the trees, barreling toward the town and pushing its massive weight into the buildings, setting them ablaze and then dropping them to the ground. Brick exploded all across town, cement turned to dust, and cars crumpled like soda cans.

"That big fucker is going to mow us down. We can't handle him." Tyler's concern appeared to be his alone. Jamie and Terrence appeared more confident of their abilities. Even becoming superhuman couldn't relieve Tyler of the doubt buried deep within him.

Jamie placed her hand on his shoulder.

"The three of us take on the lightning fire with fire style. Aluben takes the big bastard."

'Aluben?' the purple entity said in their minds.

"Nebula backwards. Heard you were born from a dead star." Terrence eyed Aluben for approval. A blank stare was all they got.

'You are correct, but I go by no name. I am just a being among the universes.'

"We fight together. You're our leader, and a leader must have a name." Jamie clenched her fists. "Lead us to battle, Aluben!"

'I will be the one who takes control of Earth. Follow, my soldiers!'

Aluben charged right toward the giant, tackling it and sending it deep into the ground.

Terrence, Tyler, and Jamie landed in town, right outside the bank. The lightning kept striking the rooftops, igniting them in scorching flames. Several people sought cover under the wreckage. Molders, who hadn't yet absorbed people, spread across the buildings, and made their way toward groups of gathered people.

"We need to help those people," Terrence said. "One of us should stand guard while the other two get them to safety."

Terrence backed up against Jamie and Tyler, forming a circle so they could get eyes all around them. The lightning didn't let up.

The three of them rotated, watching the sky. The lightning came at them from all directions.

A woman none of them recognized ran into the street. A bolt struck her, engulfing her in flames. She flailed about while screaming before finally collapsing to the ground.

"Stay here. I can get to her." Terrence moved quickly and got within a dozen yards away.

A second bolt struck her head, popping it like a swollen balloon. Fluids poured from her neck, shooting all over the street. Her waving limbs lost all strength and fell to the ground beside her.

"Fucking Christ!" Tyler felt ill after seeing that transpire.

Terrence looked up at the lightning. He raised his hand, pointed, and fired. Like the storm above him, purple bolts escaped his fingertips and fought back against the descending storm. The sky cleared as these adversaries were no match for Terrence's new power.

The lightning cleared above their heads. Jamie and Tyler's eyes were locked on to the dead woman's mangled head. Screams echoed nearby as people crowded around to see her, figuring out her identity. Terrence hovered above the town again to try to find Aluben.

"Tyler. Hey, Tyler." Jamie pulled his sleeve. "We need to get these people out of here."

"Where can we take them? We're completely surrounded by these things!"

"Grab someone. We'll find a place." Jamie floated over and wrapped her arms around the waists of a young couple, pulling them into the air. Both screamed. "Hey, not in my goddamn ear. I'm trying to help."

Tyler spotted a young mother and her son, much like how he saw himself and his own mother. He floated to them, reaching his arms out for them to come.

"Hey, let me take you out of here. I'll come back for the rest of these people once you're safe."

The mother looked at Tyler with skepticism.

"What are you?" the woman asked. "How can you fly?"

"We had a little help from the purple guy." Tyler grabbed them both and ascended high, finding Jamie in the distance and heading her way. "Jamie, wait up!"

The battle waged on. Purple beams lit the fields and the blue giant's shrieks came again and again.

Then the power in Tyler's arms weakened. His muscles, frozen in the sudden grasp from the blue giant, forced him to release the boy and woman. His muscles locked and he watched the mother as she rapidly descended back down to the ground. Tyler and the giant quickly matched their speed, but too far away to be of any help anymore.

They dropped faster and faster, and their screams made Tyler think of his own mother. Was she still alive? Had she escaped? He wasn't sure, but this sinking feeling made it hard to imagine she'd somehow survived.

Just before he and his foe hit the ground, Tyler heard the mother and son falling through the trees below, and that concerned him. The resulting thud of their bodies striking the ground crushed his heart. He was powerless to do anything, unable even to turn and face his assailant.

The blue giant released its electric grip and Tyler collapsed, defeated, free from the power he couldn't match. He struck the ground, and his body convulsed. His new powers must've given him enough strength so he didn't die, but he remained weakened by the effects of the monster's power.

He glanced at the trees, unable to locate the mother or her son. He could only imagine their agony, especially if they somehow lived through that high of a fall. There was little hope they'd survived.

Mom's probably dead, too.

A horrifying shriek rang in his ears. Lightning lit up the sky, striking all around Tyler. He had no more fight left in him. All he wanted was to find his mother. If she ended up being dead, he wasn't sure how he'd react. His father could take his place in Hell, for all he cared. But his mom… He prayed she'd made it through all this.

The shriek silenced as the sky lit with a bright purple. The blue giant tried to match the intensity, but Tyler swore he saw Terrence briefly gripping its beastly arms, keeping it still. Aluben held the giant with an immolating grip, and it was working. They were winning.

Aluben threw the giant. Terrence rushed to Tyler's aid as the blue giant crashed into the ground, the impact sending branches and dirt airborne. The debris showered Tyler and Terrence, but Tyler didn't think anything could survive a blow like that.

"Hey there, kiddo. Can you move?" Terrence was staring at Tyler's legs. Tyler hadn't even noticed the damage, but Terrence's troubled expression said it all. His legs were mangled.

"Yeah, a little." Tyler sat up, trying to get a better look. He was surprised he couldn't feel the bone protruding from his ripped jeans.

"You heal like Aluben now," Terrence said. "You're not going to feel it like you did when you were normal."

Jamie lowered herself nearby. "Tyler! Terrence! Anyone out there?"

"Over here!" Terrence shot lightning from his fingers to give his position.

Jamie rushed over.

"How are you, tough guy?" Jamie propped Tyler up on her lap. She pulled chunks of dirt from his hair. He felt at ease around them.

Tyler looked up at Terrence, pondering. "Isn't concern for people a liability?"

"That was before we were Earth's most powerful humans. Gonna need some witnesses when they make my documentary."

Aluben descended next to them. The ground rumbled as the blue giant emerged, readying itself for another round of combat.

'Humans… *Who knew they'd be my most worthy ally.*'

"Aluben, are you going to kill this thing or what? We can beat some Molder ass if you need a hand." Jamie's eyes glowed electric purple. She was ready and willing for anything coming her way.

'I fear, worthy friends, that this planet is doomed by the power it now faces. I must do the extreme to silence this vile human eater.'

Tyler tried his best to make out the words Aluben spoke but too consumed by was watching his bones snap back into place and his skin heal over like new. He flexed his muscles, standing like he was springing up from a good night's rest.

"We can all take him together. We owe it to you, our families, and everyone who's gone now." Tyler lifted his clenched fists to eye level. The fear he'd experienced to start this night was gone. Only eagerness remained, a need to redeem himself overwhelming him.

'I ask one thing of you, all of you.'

All three of them stood ready, willing to follow the extraterrestrial to the end.

'You have my powers. Watch from above the atmosphere. For your safety.'

Aluben's aura lit the darkness, consuming their surroundings. The distant stars were drowned out by the glaring purple. The blue giant looked to the light, elevating its capacity to project its horrific sound.

'The planet, like this foe, will finally come to an end. Go now.'

All three watched as Aluben hovered over to the blue monster. The shriek was brief as the crushing blow sank them both deep into the ground. They kept watching the crater's opening dug into a tunnel as their range from the scene grew further. The battle of blue and purple light gave them the view of the escalating depth. The three of them rose, watching the light dim from a distance. They admired the stars and the opportunity they wouldn't have had they not encountered Aluben.

The quiet of space swallowed them, and the silence was like nothing they had experienced before. Earth was entirely a different site from this position—more so than they'd ever expect it to be. Despite its catastrophic fate, it looked beautiful. They hadn't expected to have exceptional lives outside their quiet, boring neighborhood. Being among extraterrestrials, watching them battle, brought them all a fulfillment unlike what they knew before.

"What… What do we do now?" Tyler asked.

Terrence and Jamie looked at one another, equally lost.

The fires below grew. And then an amber glow emerged from the shifting ground and grew brighter. The lines of cracked Earth traced all across the globe, spreading in all directions like spiderwebbed glass. The three, growing fearful, felt helpless. They didn't know who was winning, despite their faith in Aluben.

Tyler's eyes filled with tears. He'd never have the closure he wanted with his parents. Not a chance in hell his life would ever be what it was before all this. No way would Earth survive this catastrophic damage.

His tears drifted off into the darkness of space. He observed the amber glow, watching it burn all he knew into extinction.

The familiar glow approached them rapidly. Aluben rose from the battlefield, charred and his arm missing. Loose flesh dangled where it should be.

'It is done.'

"What did you do?" Terrence asked.

'I killed it with fire. The heat from your planet's core.'

They watched the firework show below. The fiery lines spread faster, connecting with each other. Flashes of amber light could be seen as the magma rose. The planet crumbled before them. Unlike Aluben, Terrence, Jamie, and Tyler couldn't help but stare.

"What do we do now, Aluben?" Tyler asked.

Aluben didn't answer right away, still regenerating from the battle. A new arm emerged, greased with the innards of the slime within his decapitated shoulder. Aluben flexed, testing the recovered appendage.

'Continue on. We have other worlds to conquer.'

Terrence hovered in front of Aluben. "Hold on. Hold on. You mean to tell me you're going to let our planet burn away like an old campfire, and we're just supposed to follow you into the next galaxy?"

'It is your only option, my devoted companion.'

"You trust us? You think we're capable of doing this?" Jamie asked.

'What better destroyer is there than mankind? Come, let me show you how to be invincible.'

The four flew on, deeper into the black void. The Earth, as it burned, grew dimmer as the darkness swallowed it. Mankind had seen its final day.

ACKNOWLEDGEMENTS

To my readers, old and new, thank you for continuing support as I pursue this wild author venture. You make it all worth it. Thank you for your fearlessness.

To my (mostly horror) author friends who both inspire me and motivate me. I'm grateful that you welcome me into this bizarre world of destruction, cruelty, and mayhem. See you at cons, lunch, or the bookstore. I'm grateful for you all.

To my wife. Your love and encouragement to keep the words going is never going unnoticed. You keep my words alive, despite deterring the horrors I imagine. You free me of personal horrors.

To family and friends. The love is felt every time I start over. It helps me keep typing away. I'll never stop.

To Kenneth Cain. Thank you for taking a chance with me and encouraging me. It's an honor to have your guidance.

To Scott Cole. Your aid and creations made this process and book thrive. Thank you for your vision.

To Mom. The pillar of support. Thank you. Nothing happens without you. All my love.

ABOUT THE AUTHOR

Joseph has been writing since he was eleven years old. He was inspired by the Nickelodeon show *Doug* because he kept a journal at the same age. Since then, Joseph grew to write numerous short stories and found interest in writing screenplays.

Fast forward to his college graduation. Three short films written, produced, and directed with some film festival recognition. His love for writing stories, creating worlds, and developing characters to both admire and detest flourished as he never stopped creating.

Joseph branched off from screenplays when his ideas broadened what the screen could portray. With a collection of stories in his archive and several novels in the works, there's no telling what will come from his mind and expand onto the pages.

With each piece of writing released, Joseph is constantly expanding his creativity while interacting with fellow writers, documenting his journey, reading, and filling his mind with more inspiration for the next story.